YOU
GROW
GIRL

BELLE HENDERSON

Tamarillas Press

Cover image: Canva
Design: © Belle Henderson
Copyright © 2023 Belle Henderson

ISBN: 978-1-913807-33-7

Dedication

For Kate.
This book wouldn't exist without you and our many
talks on a dog walk. Love *Shmoo*, mate. xxx

Other books by Belle Henderson

Not The Plus One
The Hounds of Love
What's Eating Felicity Frost
Livin' La Vida Lockdown
We can Work it Out

Chapter 1

Events happened in very quick succession.

Like watching a set of dominoes come tumbling down. It took only one to fall and then everything else followed shortly after. Except watching dominoes is quite satisfying and this was more like watching your constipated dog strain for a poo then end up shitting out a pair of your best knickers. It was painful, a bit funny (if it wasn't happening to your dog) and shocking all at the same time and the worst thing was, I couldn't do anything to stop it.

The absolutely mortifying thing was, this was my life.

Brandon and I had been together for almost ten years, we had a house together in a trendy location in Coolsbay, well it was *his* house and I helped him pay the mortgage. His parents gave him a substantial deposit when we moved back home but made sure that my name wasn't on the mortgage or the deeds. I know, I still kick myself about this now.

He worked in TV, his dream job after studying at university and I think his parents persuaded him to buy a house here to stop us from moving to Bristol, where the TV company was based. Instead, he commuted an hour and a half each day but it didn't seem to bother him, said it gave him time to think. Maybe we should have moved to Bristol because his plentiful thinking time has led me to where I am today. On Fridays, Brandon and I would get a takeaway, usually Pizza, and on Saturdays we would often go out for a meal along the harbour at one of the fancy restaurants, then afterwards on to a bar for a few drinks. Well, often a few too many drinks which on occasion resulted in drunken fuelled arguments neither of us could much remember. Sometimes we met with friends, sometimes we didn't. It was nice. Life was good, comfortable and easy until it wasn't, well not for me anyway.

'Do you think we're a good match?' he asked, with his back to me as he continued to wash up, not looking back.

'Of course, the perfect match. Why do you ask?' I tilted my head, letting my brown curly hair tickle the side of my face. I wondered why he still had his back turned to me? Why he didn't look at me when he asked, or when I answered?

I stared at his muscled forearms as they continued to flex as he washed up in our/his Belfast ceramic sink. His cheek length dark hair which was once very long and wavy, swished in time to his movement. We were, at least I thought we were, a very good match.

We met at university in Manchester and we were both studying media, me music and him TV. Even though we were from the same town, we hadn't properly met until then. I'd seen him about, of course, as Coolsbay is a very small town. He was very easy on the eye with full lips, thick, long surfer-dude hair, dark brown eyes and a strong, athletic build. I'd never had the guts to strike up a conversation with him here, so, when he came up to me in the student bar on the first night of university saying that he recognised me, I was ecstatic.

Within two weeks, after many a drunken, deep and meaningful conversation, and plenty of hungry student sex, we were a firm couple. There's always that one couple that get together in freshers' week and end up staying together forever. An unbreakable bond, fused by suddenly becoming a grownup and finding out that you want exactly the same things. You've definitely met your drinking match but also your soul mate. It was meant to be. That was us.

Or at least I thought it was.

'Oh, I don't know, just wondered. Forget I said anything, Pudding,' he said.

'Okay.'

But I couldn't forget. For the next week I badgered him about it, probably a little too much. He kept saying it was nothing, I was being silly. Until one day, when he was drying the dishes, he said, 'I've bought tickets for a round the world trip.'

My eyes fell to his forearms again and I watched as the muscles tensed and untense with each wipe of the cloth. My heart was in my mouth. He'd bought us tickets to travel the world together, could life get any better? But what about my job? I guess I'd have to tell my dickhead of a boss to do one, that wouldn't be so hard. Enjoyable even. I'm PA to the senior manager in one of the biggest banks in town and I loathe him. My mind started to wander, fantasising about the many countries we'd visit and the tasty cuisine and scenery we'd get to discover. This was perfect, just what we needed. A bit of adventure away from the boredom of our home town where we knew everyone and every place like the back of our hands. Yes, it would be nice to be strangers in a strange place.

'What? This is amazing, but how can we afford it? Did you get a summer bonus and not tell me?' I screeched with excitement as he turned around with his mouth open. Why had all the colour drained from his face? Why wasn't he excited like me? 'I knew that new TV series was going to take off,' I continued, still screeching. 'What's it called again? Will you be filming abroad then?' I asked, trying to make sense of it all, my voice trailing off as I noticed his contorted expression.

'Oh God, no,' he snapped. 'Look, I've taken a sabbatical. What I mean is, I've bought myself tickets. I'm going, Lottie. I need to go and see the world for a bit, experience new cultures, new people. Everything has gone a bit stagnant recently and I need to spread my wings, just for a while. I'm still so young.' He hung up the tea towel as my hand flew up to my mouth. He always did the washing *and* drying up, even if we both cooked, he was good like that. He was kind, respectful and apparently a huge selfish bastard too, despite the washing and drying up.

'What do you mean?' I whimpered as my throat began to throb.

'I'm going, alone, to see the big wide world.' He nodded as his eyebrows knitted together. I watched his dark hair bounce around on top of his head and I focussed on it, deciding it very much resembled a helmet as I tried to come to terms with what he was telling me.

'But what about us? You and me?' I squeaked, blinking back burning tears.

'I need to do this alone,' he said, agitated as he began to stack the plates, the posh ones that his mum gave us. His pride and joy. I hated them. They were twee with little birds on, fragile and expensive and we only got them out every Sunday, like an old married couple. I guess he was right, we were a bit stagnant.

'But, but, but when? How long?' A strangled voice managed to escape me. He looked at me with something in his eyes I hadn't seen before in the entire time we had been together, pity. It was pity.

'Next week. I leave in a week's time and I'll be gone for at least six months. I'm sorry.'

'No, you're not.' I shook my head and looked away, a throbbing painful lump now fully formed in my throat.

'You can stay here until the end of July but then you'll need to find somewhere else as I'll be renting it out via an estate agent, Mum and Dad have strongly advised I do this so I'm afraid my hands are tied.'

I couldn't believe what I was hearing, last night we went to our favourite restaurant then met with a friend for drinks. Then after eating a very nice roast cooked by me, he told me he's going on an around-the-world trip and not only is he leaving me behind, he's leaving me homeless. Never have I kicked myself so hard for not putting more pressure on him to add me to the mortgage. I deserved to be on the mortgage and the deeds; I've contributed for the entire time he's owned this house, which is almost nine years. But what hurts more is that he's had this all planned out. But for how long?

'So that's it then? You're breaking up with me and buggering off on a year's holiday without me,' I croaked.

'A minimum of six months,' he corrected. 'I need to go and see what else is out there, you get that don't you, Lottie?' He looked at me with a grimace, pleadingly almost. He wanted fresh, he wanted fun and apparently, I wasn't giving that to him anymore.

'Oh yeah, I get it alright,' I mumbled to the back of

his head, as he retreated into the living room to call his parents and report back to them that he'd done the deed. I bet they were most pleased because they never did like me. I've been called grumpy and tempestuous over the years by his father on many occasions just because I didn't laugh at his awful, sexist jokes. They really didn't want me as a daughter-in-law. I wouldn't be surprised if this is all their suggestion.

Brandon can be easily led.

The next few hours, weeks and days were a bit of a blur. I remember the twee plates smashing and Brandon shouting and screaming that his toe was cut but I don't remember exactly how it happened. I assume it was me, it had to be but I just can't remember the how. For the next few days, I phoned in sick to work and when I eventually returned my boss was there waiting for me with a face like thunder. There was no, are you okay? No concern, just a bombardment of orders that I was expected to follow as his PA/servant/dogsbody.

'Lottie, finally you're back.' My boss boomed. He stood way too close to me with his foul coffee breath and cheese and onion smelling armpits. 'I'm completely snowed under, I need a conference organising asap, flowers sending and minutes taking in a meeting in five minutes. Not to mention the amount of filing and other general admin that has piled up all because you fancied taking a few days off due to your MENTAL HEALTH.' His voice got louder and higher at the end of the sentence. He was so unfit that the long sentence and effort of speaking loudly had left him visibly panting. I took a few steps back away from his attempt at belittling me and the smell of his deep-fried armpits.

'That's nice,' I said sarcastically, with a forced smile that felt like it was taking over my entire face. I flicked my hair behind my shoulders and grinned again but this time it was genuine. It was almost as if I was auditioning for the main character in a film and this was her moment to finally be true to herself.

'Excuse me?' he said, as his already ham coloured face turned a deeper shade of puce and steam visibly left his ears – or at least that's how it seemed to me.

'That's nice because it's nice to be busy, isn't it?' I leant forward slightly to flick his tie. 'I hope you enjoy your tasks because there'll be plenty of them, oh and by the way you smell of crisps and not the nice flavours,' I continued as I watched his jaw and fists clench in unison. 'I'll be off then, bye.' And with that, I stupidly and manically skipped out of the building.

Relationshipless, homeless and now jobless.

Chapter 2

Hi gang,

So this marks month five of my round the world trip and I can honestly say that I'm having the time of my life. I'm currently in Thailand on a boat on my way over to a full moon party. Living the dream. Life couldn't be better. Fact.

Click on the link below to view my new blog post where I detail my experience of Patpong and the lovely ladies that inhabit it.

www.wherebrandonboldlygoes.co.uk

Peace x

P.S. I am not a sex tourist haha.

I file away Brandon's email on my phone and silently congratulate myself for doing so. I'm done with reading his generic emails and blog posts. It's not good for me. It stings that he couldn't be bothered to send me a personal email but what's worse is that he hasn't answered my replies to his generic ones. France, Spain, Turkey, India and now Thailand and not even one lousy postcard or personal email to me in the whole five months he's been away. If that doesn't scream *I don't care* then I don't know what does. I drop my phone into my handbag and stare out of the window of Aloe Lovely, my friend's plant shop, where I now work part-time.

'But he just looks so sad,' I say to Willow, as she stops watering the philodendron to see who I'm staring at.

Narrowing my eyes to get a better look, I peer over the yucca as I watch the lonely homeless man who's been sitting there since I started work this morning at ten am. It's almost three pm now and it appears this man has taken up a new residency upon the steps of Coolsbay shopping centre.

'I mean it's not the best place to set up camp is it? And he looks freezing,' I continue, as I sit down, sigh, then rest my chin on my hands. The homeless man attempts to wrap himself up into his thin rain jacket before blowing on his hands to try and warm them. He doesn't make any attempt to catch the eyes of the public to beg for money. Instead, he just stares glumly at the pavement, watching what remains of the winter leaves dance about in the wind.

'He does look cold, the poor thing. I don't think we have any spare blankets either; I gave them all to the local dog charity. He doesn't even have a hat.' Willow's eyebrows draw together before she sprays the leaves of the monstera, frantically cleaning the dust off it in the hope that today will be its lucky day of finally finding an owner.

The plant has been with Willow since she opened the shop last year, she wants to sell it but she's also become quite attached to it. Almost like it's an old friend. Willow and I have only known each other for five years; we met when we worked at Coolsbay Associates together and have stayed in touch ever since. When I needed a job, Willow was the first and only person to offer. It was really handy when I walked out of my job and needed something a bit gentler. Since we met, Willow has achieved many wonderful things such as opening up this beautiful plant shop Aloe Lovely and I have… well, I've plodded along not really getting anywhere and often drinking a few wines of an evening to forget my sad sorry life.

I've never really minded just being a plodder, except now I'm suddenly thirty-one, without my own home, a partner or a full-time job. I also have a university reunion coming up and I'm feeling an overwhelming sense of pressure to not look like a complete failure at life. Plus, *he's* probably going to be there. Brandon. I'd be lying if I said I didn't at least want him to want me back. There's perhaps a tiny part of me that wants him back too. I know it's shameful, but you'd want your old life back if you'd lost all your friends and home comforts. Brandon and I had loads of couple-mates but when he went off travelling, they were quick to ditch me after I said I didn't fancy going out much anymore. Alcohol certainly wasn't a great friend when he first left so I've recently tried to cut back on that and now my only true friend is Willow, not counting my family of course.

'I have loads of hats, I certainly don't need them all,' I muse, as I rummage around underneath the desk for a hat. I find a bright red one then twirl it round in my hands, studying the Christmas pudding that's been knitted into the front of it. Homeless man isn't going to care that it's a silly novelty hat, is he? He'll just want to keep his head warm. Plus, Brandon gave it to me, it's probably time to let go of it and that terrible nickname now, who wants to be known as a *pudding* anyway.

Not me.

Stuff the pudding.

Perhaps this is step one of letting go.

Homeless man won't mind that it's January and no one wants to be reminded of anything remotely Christmassy anymore. 'He's not eaten or drunk a thing since I noticed him this morning, God knows how long it's been since he's had a meal. Maybe he's just left the army and has nowhere else to go now,' I say, feeling suddenly very sorry for this man and the make-believe backstory I've just created for him.

'Hmmmm, he looks quite well looked after though,' Willow muses, as she peers through the window, rearranging the display whilst surreptitiously inspecting him scrolling on his phone. But everyone has a phone these days, even the homeless. 'He's definitely had a shave in the last few days so he must have stayed somewhere and he's not begging for money so perhaps he's alright?' She shrugs. As her big mirrored earrings jangle around her they shine triangle lights onto her face.

'Not many people are just alright, Willow. Trust me. I should know.' I stand up gripping the hat with one hand as I reach for my handbag with the other, certain about what I'm going to do next. It's the right thing to do. It's the only thing I *can* do. 'I'll be right back.' The shop door jangles like Willow's earrings as I dash through it and past the homeless man to the small corner shop at the end of the high street.

'Lottie, my beautiful Italian rose.' Ravi beams as I bustle into his shop that really only has room for two people at once, maximum. It's like stepping into someone's large broom cupboard, but I love it and Ravi is lovely too. He sells the best pickled gherkins and also gives the best life advice.

'Hey Ravi, you know I'm an English rose, I'm only a quarter Italian on my dad's side.'

'Yes, but all that beautiful dark curly hair is certainly the Italian part, my beauty. You have hair like stunning brown poodle dog.' He smiles and wibbles his head slightly. I smile back at him.

'Thanks Ravi, I can always rely on you for the original compliments,' I say, as I scour the shop for a sandwich, crisps, a chocolate bar and a drink for the homeless man. I take three freshly cooked vegetable samosas from the counter, the heat immediately warming my hands and my mouth watering for the spicy goodness. 'Can I have all of that please?' I ask Ravi. 'I'm just going to grab one more thing, quickly.' I dash to the coffee machine and make the homeless man a strong coffee, that will warm him up a bit too and the caffeine will get his nervous system going, I'm sure. I'm doing a good thing. My good deed of the day and I won't be posting it on social media and demanding praise for it either. I'm simply paying it forward and doing something nice for someone in need. Just because I've been shat on from a huge height doesn't mean I should do the same to others. Think nice thoughts, do nice things, be a good person.

That is my new mantra.

I'm not the grumpy person that Brandon's dad thinks I am.

I've finally turned a corner.

'That will be £12.69 please my lovely,' Ravi says, as I hover my card over the card machine. 'Ooops, card declined.' Ravi frowns and sticks his bottom lip out.

'Oh shit, but it can't have done, there must be something wrong with the machine?' I point at it accusingly.

'We'll try again.' Ravi smiles and nods his head.

'Always something wrong with temperamental stupid machine.'

'Thanks, Ravi,' I smile through the lump forming in my throat. I can't have spent all my money already, can I? I mentally tally up my big spends since last pay day and doom darkens my soul as I remember the amount of times I've paid to have my online tarot cards read this month. Too many. Way too many. I may have cut the alcohol down but my addictive and impulsive personality sometimes runs away with me in other ways.

'Oops no, card is really declined, Lottie. Try another card?'

'Ummm, I don't have another.' I do but it's my savings card that I have been so careful not to touch for years and it's at home, at least I have that. I was saving up to surprise Brandon with a lump sum to put towards the house but it could have also been spent on travelling with him, except he didn't want me to come. My mind jumps to Brandon's emails and the blog posts I've read, studied and obsessed over for the past five months. Potentially there's only one more to go and then he could be home, although one of his emails did say he might extend his stay to a year, so who knows.

'Okay, we try again,' Ravi says, as another customer enters the shop and my cheeks turn the same colour as the Christmas pudding hat. Ravi shakes his head. 'No worries my lovely,' he whispers. 'We do I.O.U, just pay me next time.' He winks and nods his head and the lump appearing in my throat begins to throb as I watch him, through blurry eyes, put everything into a bag.

'Are you sure?' I squeak.

'I insist. The generous will always be returned with generosity.'

'Thank you,' I manage before grabbing the coffee and

leaving the shop. I'll pay him back as soon as I can. I'm sure I've got about £20 in cash at home.

Must check my online banking and see what the hell's gone on. But first, I need to pay it forward or is that backwards because I've not actually paid for it?

As I approach the shopping centre, I spot the homeless man still sitting on the steps, looking as fed up as he did before, blowing warm air into his hands to try and stop them from freezing. I wonder what happened for him to end up here. It's so easy for a series of events to leave you vulnerable and if it wasn't for Willow letting me work in her shop part-time and my brother letting me live in his house rent free, I guess I could be in a very similar position. With coffee in one hand and a bag of goodies in the other I arrange my face into a kind yet sympathetic expression.

'Hey, I hope you don't mind but I thought you could use these,' I say, gently, passing him the coffee and the bag of goodies. He looks in the bag and frowns.

'Oh, why?' he grumbles. Well, that wasn't the response I was expecting.

'Umm, because you look cold and hungry and you've been here quite a while,' I say tentatively, as I take my pudding hat off and give it to him. 'I work in Aloe Lovely and couldn't help but notice you,' I point to the shop, so he doesn't think I'm a complete stalker.

'Right, I see,' homeless man says, studying the hat. To my surprise he puts it on the pavement then studies the contents of the bag.

'Okay, well I hope this helps. It's a small gesture I know but it's all I can afford. You should wear the hat, it's cold today.' I smile then realise I'm standing there awkwardly, just watching him. He slowly puts on the hat and gives me the thumbs up. 'Have a nice day,' I continue. Oh no I shouldn't have said that, it won't be nice of course. He's homeless.

'Thanks love,' he says taking a bite of the samosa and I kick myself for not taking the other two out which I bought for mine and Willow's lunch. He can have them though, he's homeless after all, I can hardly take food back off a homeless man. 'Wow this samosa is good. Got any sugar for the coffee, love?'

'No sorry, I don't.' The phrase *beggars can't be choosers* pops into my mind before I can stop myself from thinking it. Damn you, intrusive thoughts. 'Enjoy.' I beam before turning on my heel to head back to work.

Good deed of the day done. Tick.

Willow stops what she's doing to the window display and tilts her head, watching me pad back to the shop with a big satisfied grin on my face. She squints her eyes at me then arranges her mouth into a smirk-like smile.

'That guy,' she says, pointing a finger behind me. 'Is he definitely homeless?'

'Yes of course he is, why?' I say, as I turn around to see what she's pointing at. Homeless man or should I say, potentially fake homeless man, has stood up and is talking to a woman holding copious amounts of shopping bags. It appears they know each other very well. He reluctantly takes the shopping bags from her before they exchange a bit of a heated discussion as she points at the hat on his head. I take in his clothes again, grey rain jacket, slightly ripped jeans, tidy trainers. Then my eyes fall to her as they continue to bicker. She's wearing a pink rain jacket, jeans and designer trainers. They both have wedding rings on and matching jackets but in different colours. Realisation sets in.

'That's his bloody wife, isn't it?' I groan as my hand hits my head.

'I think it could be, yes,' Willow says slowly, as she bites her lip and a snort-like sound escapes her.

'How dare he.' I march back out of the shop right up to the couple and stand between them with my hands on my hips.

'Who are you?' The wife squawks.

'So you're not homeless,' I boom, ignoring the wife's question.

'I never said I was, you mad girl,' he protests, as his wife eyeballs us both.

'You might be if you carry on sulking like a teenager,' wife pipes up.

'I thought he was homeless so I bought him a coffee and some food and I gave him my hat,' I say evenly, as I point to the Christmas pudding hat sitting on his head.

'Craig!' The woman gasps, snatching the hat off his head and passing it to me. 'You know he's been sitting out here for the entire shopping trip,' she says, as her eyes meet mine. 'Would rather sit out in the cold than mooch around a few shops with me, his poor wife. Sad, isn't it?'

'That's why I thought he was homeless; he's been out here for hours.' I nod wide eyed.

'Urgh women. You can't win. Us men can never do anything right. All I wanted was a bit of peace and quiet and this happens, I've got two women giving me grief instead of one,' fake homeless man whines.

'No, you can't win, because in reality you're all just lying, selfish cheating shits,' I say, as the wife gasps again and I realise my faux pas. 'No, sorry *he* hasn't cheated, not to my knowledge anyway,' I add, eyeing him with disgust. 'I'm just speaking from my own experience, well not the cheating bit I don't think, but who really knows. Anyway, I've got what I wanted.' I hold up the bag of food and my hat, which I really don't want back. 'You can keep the coffee. Good day.'

I turn on my heel, stomping back to the shop and leave the couple to argue it out. Story of my life, being nice just gets chucked back in my face time and time again, I'm best off being a grump. As I open the door to the shop, Craig the fake homeless man, shouts after me.

'Oi, it's not us men, it's you women. You assume stuff when you should just ask us. AND you normally assume the worst, just like *you* did. You never asked if I was bloody homeless.'

I don't turn back and respond, instead his words ring in my ears as I dump the stupid pudding hat in the bin and retrieve the samosas out of the shopping bag. Willow gives me a sympathetic grimace and hands me a freshly made cup of tea and a pickled gherkin.

I ignore Craig, the fake homeless man.

He'll have to assume I didn't hear him.

Chapter 3

There's probably only one man who I don't think is a complete twonk today and that's my brother, Harry.

Oh no, Dad's cool too. Sorry Dad.

But all jokes aside, I really do adore my brother. He's sweet, kind and an all-round fun guy to be around. Plus, he's so laid back he's almost horizontal. He never minded me just turning up to bend his ear or eat all his food and in the early days when I was back living with Mum and Dad, I did this so often that eventually they staged an intervention and suggested that I live with him until I get a place of my own. They all decided it was better for my well-being if I went and lived with Harry. I think the real reason is that Mum and Dad were fed up with listening to me and my teenage sister squabble like a couple of kids. God, I sound more like Harry's child than his sister and there's only four years between us.

How utterly depressing.

I step off the bus and make the ten-minute walk down to Harry's house. He lives right by the sea in a little light-blue two up two down house with a balcony that just about accommodates a tiny table and two chairs. It's my happy place and my spirits have lifted slightly since living here. The views of Coolsbay from the twee balcony are just stunning. These days, to cheer myself up, I quite often watch the crashing of the waves coupled with the seagulls circling around unsuspecting tourists' heads. Recently, I saw a gull swipe a whole Mr Whippy ice cream from someone's hand before dropping the remains on the next tourist's head. The gull, you see, had seen a better offer from someone else in the form of a cone of chips. Of course, the gull wasn't offered the chips, he stole them. The tourists always make me laugh, they're so trusting of the Coolsbay seagulls and I know they can be ballsy in Cornwall and Devon but here in Coolsbay just a smidge east of Devon, they're bigger, greedier and much cheekier.

'Harry!' I squeal, as I wave at him from across the road. He closes the navy-blue door behind him before checking the road and holding up his big shovel-like hand to wave back at me. My brother and I are very similar in looks, we both have big curly brown hair and brown eyes. The big difference is that he is well over six foot tall and I'm a short arse at just five-foot-two. He'd argue that he has better curls than me and I'd argue that his just look better because they're shorter hence less weight to drag them down.

'Oh hey, Lottie, I'm just off out but I'll be back in a couple of hours.'

'Oh, okay, where are you going?'

'Just over the road for a couple of games of pool with the boys, come if you like?'

'Oh no, I'll just stay in and eat you out of house and home, that alright?'

'Yeah, sure, everything alright?' he asks, putting his hand on my shoulder.

'Yeaaah, just had a bit of a shit day,' I say, shaking my head as the image of the fake homeless man in my

Christmas pudding hat pops into my mind.

'Thought so, listen, I won't be long okay? You can tell me all about it when I'm back.' He holds out his hand for a fist bump.

'Thanks, bro,' I say fist bumping him back.

'Don't eat my Mars bars.' He points at me before turning around and taking long strides down the path. 'Oh and Kathy's home, be nice.'

'I'll try not to,' I say, as my brother glares at me. 'I mean I'll try not to eat your Mars bars. Of course I'll be nice to Kathy. She's great,' I lie. She isn't that great, in fact she's quite the annoying housemate that turned into my brother's girlfriend and now won't ever leave. I have no reason not to like her, except for that very reason. I know that makes me a bitch but I'm allowed to be a bitch, I'm heartbroken and I don't want love rubbed in my face, okay? The sound of their sex screams are almost too much to bear, I'm his sister and it makes me feel physically sick. The screams don't match the Kathy when she's not having sex either.

'Hey, helllooooooo,' I call out, as I enter the house and wait for the high-pitched squeal that belongs to Kathy.

'Hey Sis,' she replies from the living room. I wince at the over familiarity. They've been dating for four months for God's sake. We're hardly sisters. Just mere acquaintances that have been thrown together because we share the company of someone close to us. Step-sisters might be a more suitable term for this relationship. I might start referring to her as Steppy.

'What's your goss, Kathy?' I ask in an attempt to 'be nice.' She's sitting on her new, precious sofa doing a crossword and no she's not sixty-seven, she's my age.

'Oh, you know I don't do gossip, Lottie, and neither should you,' she says, as she continues to scribble on the page. 'What's another word for victim, prey? Six letters?' Crossword she's doing a crossword.

'I dunno, loser?'

'Lottie!'

'No, I didn't mean it like that, but if they're prey they've lost haven't they? Hence a loser?'

'No, and it's 5 letters, not 6. Anyway, do *you* have any news?' Kathy asks, as she looks down the end of her glasses at me which, if they were any further down the end of her nose would fall off into her mouth.

'News. Isn't that just another word for gossip?' I ponder, whilst playing with one of the many doilies that have appeared on all the surfaces in the house. Honestly, I thought only eighty-year-olds had doilies in their houses.

'No. News is news, like what you learnt about yourself today or perhaps learning that a new planet has been discovered or a new species of ant. Not bone-idle chit chat about other people.' She nods to herself and I force my face into a smile. Be nice.

'Well in that case no, I have no news,' I say, thinking about the fake homeless man and his wife and how kindness was thrown back in my face. My mind then drifts to my bank card declining in Ravi's shop and a groan escapes me.

'Oooh, what's that? Thought of something?' Kathy sits up straight in her seat, looking very much like an over-alert meerkat, seemingly way more excited than she should be about my potential bad *news*.

'No, no,' I lie. 'Just really tired, I might just go and lie down for a bit.'

'Okay,' she sings and I leave the room, the doilies and the grandma to complete her crossword. I make my way to the kitchen and after searching the cupboards for a good few minutes, feeling frustrated at the copious amounts of Kathy's non-descript cardboard diet food I have to sift through. I settle for a cup of tea and three Jammie Dodger biscuits. That will do nicely.

Bang. Bang. Bang.

The door shakes from behind the very insistent knocker. I tiptoe into the corridor and wait in the hallway just out of view of the window.

Bang. Bang. Bang.

'Coming.' I sing loudly, in the hope that Kathy will come and answer the door and shoo this person away. I'm not in the mood for people today, not any more anyway.

I peer into the living room and Grandma, surprise, surprise, is asleep. Kathy is what Brandon would describe as a mouth breather. I watch as her slack jawline caused by the mouth breathing, disappears into her chin, getting deeper with every breath she takes. I wonder if she'd appreciate the information I learnt about mewing recently from a VERY chatty customer. Apparently mouth breathing can cause bad breath and sleep apnoea. Who knew?

Bang. Bang. Bang.

'COMING,' I boom, before setting my Jammie Dodgers down on the floor so I have a spare hand. The figure stands in front of the door impatiently pacing from side to side. It's probably a sales guy wanting to sell guttering or something. They're so pushy these days.

'Can I help?' I ask in what I hope is my stern voice as I open the door just a smidge.

'Lottie, little Grotty Lottie,' the figure says and I groan inwardly. There's only one person who calls me that, Liam, my brother's best friend and the bane of my life.

'Urgh, you're back,' I say, not stepping back to let him

in. His blue eyes twinkle mockingly in the winter sun and I notice he has a tan, quite a dark one too. 'You look like a burnt gingerbread man,' I say, eyeing him up and down. He has a full face of fuzz too, which almost matches the tone of his skin.

'Nice welcome back, Grotty.' He laughs. 'So, where's the main man?'

'He's out, playing pool, should be back soon, shall I tell him you called by?' I say, as I begin to close the door on him. Not in the mood today. I'm all peopled out.

'Nah,' he says using his foot as a wedge to keep the door open. 'I'll just wait for him, he must have forgotten. You know what he's like. Be a nice surprise now, won't it? I've been gone a while. Plus, *we* have a lot of catching up to do.'

'Do we?'

'Sure,' he says in a sing songy voice which highlights the Irish accent that has faded slightly but never gone away completely. A flashback of us as teenagers and Liam playing many a practical joke on me slides into my mind. He loved winding me up and one time, he thought it would be funny to put cat biscuits in my cereal. Unknowingly I ate them, as they blended into the cereal perfectly. It was then that the nickname Grotty was born, because as soon as he told me I puked into the cereal bowl and it was pure grottiness.

I reluctantly step back and let him in. Liam has always been a bit of a prat, he was like the annoying middle brother that I never wanted. He was always at our house, that is until he and my brother grew apart for a bit. He pads along the corridor towards the living room until I hear a crunching sound.

'Oh shit,' he says. 'Who left them there?'

My eyes fall to the Jammy Dodgers on the floor which

are now smashed into a thousand pieces. I look up to the ceiling and sigh.

'You've got to admit that was pretty stupid, leaving them there.' He points to the mess with a smirk on his face and I shake my head.

'It was pretty stupid of you to not look where you're going.'

'Now now, Grotty, don't get all snotty with me, I've only been back five minutes. Where's my hug?'

'Already feels like forever,' I say, as I push off his bear hug and usher him into the kitchen to fetch a dustpan and brush. Also I don't fancy introducing him to a Nanna Napping Kathy, I'll let my brother do the honours there. 'You can start making the teas while I tidy up,' I order, as he begins to scour the cupboards for teabags.

'Two sugars?'

'Yes please,' I say, as I arrive back in the kitchen with the crumbs that were meant to be my snack.

'How was it then?' I ask, not being able to help my curiosity. Liam has been out to Northern Ireland apparently helping disadvantaged teens before flying out to Thailand to do the same thing.

'It was brilliant, heart wrenching, humbling, emotional but brilliant. I'd do it all again in a heartbeat.'

'Why don't you then?' I ask with a straight face, not sure who this version of Liam is any more.

'I have responsibilities here with my house and stuff,' he says, as he bites into one of Kathy's diet cardboardesque breakfast bars. He chews tentatively before making a face.

'Ahh right,' I say, not wanting to ask him what *and stuff* is.

'I'll probably go back out there again soon though,

once I've sorted a few things here and spread the Irish joy and charm. Who knows! The world is my oyster, Grotty.'

'I'm sure they have enough joy and charm in Ireland and Thailand without you spreading yours,' I say, as my thoughts turn to my ex and what he might be doing right now. I can only imagine it isn't charity work.

'So, how's Big Dickhead?' he asks, as though reading my thoughts.

'Who?' I ask, almost choking on another Jammy Dodger.

'You know, Big Dickhead Energy? That's what he used to call himself at football.'

'Hmm, it was Big Dick Energy and I honestly don't know how he is. He left me five months ago, to go off travelling.' I shrug and look out of the kitchen window. Five months ago I was living with the love of my life who used to joke he had big dick energy, he wasn't up himself really, far from it. He was a good laugh, not only that, he was sexy, clever and thoughtful and kind. All of those things. He did the washing *and* the drying up. I really thought I'd hit the jackpot. We talked of plans to move to a big city like London or Manchester eventually but for the time being we were happy being in our little bubble in Coolsbay. I had a good job, a healthy bank balance and I was just starting to see two tiny abs forming from all the working out I was doing. I was getting in shape for a long-awaited proposal. A proposal that sadly never came. Life was good though, it was comfortable, I was comfortable and he was well, just bored, I guess.

'Oh, right, sorry.' Liam's eyebrows knit together and I notice his eyebrows have been bleached by the sun. They remind me of a fluffy tabby cat.

'Yeah, it's fine. He used the typical *needs to find himself* cliché line on me and then he was gone the next week. Pooooff.' I theatrically throw my arms up in the air to symbolise his leaving and Liam nods his head, pursing his lips together disapprovingly.

'Ah, he wants to fuck loads of other girls before he settles down, you mean?' He nods slowly.

'Probably.' I wince. 'Who cares.' I scowl.

'You? How long were you together?'

'Over ten years and no, I don't care,' I lie, then press my lips together because it's actually devastated me and my whole life has seemingly fallen apart ever since.

'Okay,' Liam says, sensing my discomfort. We sit in silence for the next few minutes, finishing our cups of tea and avoiding eye contact.

'So, what do you plan to do for work whilst you're back?' I ask, changing the subject away from *my* sad sorry life.

'Oh, you know, this and that. Just odd jobs and stuff. I can do anything, handyman, me,' he says, jiggling his hands in the air as if he's just finished a jazz dance.

Despite myself I laugh.

'Murphy! How is my main man?' My brother grins as he appears from behind me with his arms outstretched.

'Pricey, how's it going mate?' Liam gets up with an equally as goofy grin on his face and gives my brother a big bear hug. They slap each other on the back a few times whilst laughing and commenting on how it's been way too long and how great the other looks. In the meantime, Kathy has appeared in the kitchen door way, looking the opposite of pleased.

'And who is this lovely lady?' Liam schmoozes, holding his arm to take Kathy's hand. Despite her previous sour face, her scowl melts away and she giggles girlishly, giving him her hand. He sickeningly kisses it then twizzles her around. Liam always has to go on the charm offensive.

'I'm Kathy, Harry's girlfriend,' she says, clearing her throat. 'And I also live here.' She shakes her mousy brown bob then looks at Liam pointedly, clearly letting him know that she is not open for doily inspections. He grins and nods as his eyes move to my brother.

'Pricey, you dark horse, how could you keep this lovely lady secret from me?'

My brother, who is not easily flustered, looks a little uncomfortable.

'Did I?' he says, sounding a little off key as Kathy eyeballs him.

'Nah, but that's okay, we have plenty of time to get to know each other, especially as I'll be here all the time now.' Liam shrugs then takes a bite of the diet breakfast bar, before remembering it's disgusting and pulls a *yuk* face. Kathy turns a deep shade of beetroot.

'Here all the time?' she squeaks.

'Yep,' my brother says, grimacing as he suddenly realises his HUGE mistake. He puts a hand on Kathy and Liam's backs and looks at me pointedly. 'Kathy, Lottie, this is Liam, our new housemate.'

'Oh,' Kathy and I squawk in unison.

'What? You're moving in here?' I hear myself say.

'Yep, just till I get back on my feet. The tenants in my house have six months' notice so I couldn't boot them out before then, could I?'

'Six months, you're going to be here for six months?' I say slowly whilst furtively glancing at my brother who is mouthing *sorry* at me.

'Yeah, Grotty, so you'll be pleased to know, you're going to be seeing loads more of me.'

'Oh lovely,' I mutter unenthusiastically, as Kathy catches my eye and shakes her head. There are only two bedrooms. Kathy and Harry share one and I have the other. Looks like I'll be going back to Mum and Dad's to argue with my hormonal teenage sister again.

Great.

Scratch my previous declaration; Harry is now also a twonk.

Chapter 4

NextlevelNyssa
In order to level up you must let go of who you used to be and be
prepared to go through a period of difficult transitions. Lean in to
feeling uncomfortable, embrace it, after all growth only comes after
pain. I want you to do something for me. Write down three things
that you would like to manifest this year. Then write down why you
don't deserve them. Trust the process. It won't be easy but it will be
worthwhile, I promise. Love & light, Nyssa xx

Laying in my old bedroom back at my parents' house, I
stare up at my battered Justin Timberlake poster that's
been stuck on the wall since 2007. The poster that can
never come off as Mum and Dad will then discover that
I used chewing gum to keep it up for all these years. I'm
surprised they've kept my room this way or my younger
sister Maggie hasn't stolen it, maybe they always knew I
would come back and forth like a bloody yo-yo.

How depressing.

My eyes fall back to my phone and I whack a like on
NextLevelNyssa's post as I ponder on the three things
that I really want from my life now that I've hit the ripe
old age of thirty-one with exactly zero prospects.
Scrolling through the rest of her photos and previous

posts, it seems Nyssa is quite the private person. You only see the back of her head, a long sleek black bob and sometimes a perfectly formed angular shoulder or a manicured hand resting on a notebook. Nyssa likes pointy nails in bright colours; today they are painted neon green with a combination of white and neon pink swirls carefully painted over the top. She's an enigma. An enigma that has 100k followers all telling her how wonderful she is and how she has changed many lives. I'm a sucker for stuff like this, especially fortune tellers, in particular tarot readers which always seem to tell me exactly what I sort of want to hear followed by a bit of what I think is much needed advice. But maybe I need the opposite as that clearly isn't working and it's also costing me way too much money, eating away at my savings. Which reminds me, I must pop in to pay Ravi back for my seemingly pointless act of kindness that was thrown back in my face.

Whilst musing about what three things I would like to happen this year, I try to remember how I ended up following her or where she came from. I can't, but deciding which three things I want to happen is quite easy, well a non-brainer really because recently it's all I can think about. I feel underneath my pillow for my notebook of sad scribbles and jot down the words from NextLevelNyssa's post as well as my three desirable things.

1. *Own my own home – I really need my own space more than ever*
2. *Find my purpose – or at least a full-time job that I like – I can't sponge off of Willow forever. I'm not sure if she even needs a part-time shop assistant. I don't deserve this because I'm a flaky person who never finds joy in work.*

3. *Get Brandon back – and make his parents see that I'm*
   worthy of him. I am worthy of him.

I quickly wipe a tear away that's snuck out of my eye and decide to stop this delving into self-reflection as I appear to be destroying any ounce of self-worth I had left. I look up into Justin Timberlake's eyes, was he even the perfect man we all thought he was? I doubt it. An email pops up from Ziggy, my old uni pal and I click on it, thankful for the much-needed distraction away from my sorry life but it doesn't last long.

Hey party people,

I am beyond excited to see each and every one of you imminently. Just a reminder that the reunion is soon, I've attached the invite with hotel details and the date. Partners/husbands/wives are still very much welcome if you so wish but no kids as we want you to have fun and let your hair down like the old days, not wipe up snot and tell off your little crotch goblins (which I'm sure they aren't.) It's been ten years so we all have a lot of catching up to do. Let me know if you have any questions . . . and before I go . . .remember this . . .

> *Hall four, hall four*
> *Move out of my way*
> *Hall four, hall four*
> *We're here to play*
> *Hall four, hall four*
> *Don't hate, just cheer.*
> *Hall four, hall four*
> *Let's go, more beer.*
> *Spartacus campus for life!*
> *Peace out! The Zig monster xx*

Oh shit. The Uni reunion in Manchester. Back when I booked the hotel everything was hunky dory and Brandon was coming too. I don't know if I can face it right now but I was so looking forward to seeing everyone, especially Kate and Lydia my closest pals at the time. After Brandon and I got together and moved back to Coolsbay, I saw my uni friends less and less. He was so focused on forging a career in TV that I just fell into step with him, travelling with him to interviews and almost becoming his roadie. Plus we all live so far away from each other that it's difficult to meet up when real life keeps getting in the way. My thoughts turn to Kate and Lydia and all the fun we used to have; it would be so lovely to see them again. I should go. I should force myself to go – push the boundaries, step out of my comfort zone. Get uncomfortable in my own skin and just embrace it, just like NextlevelNyssa would say to do. Also, there's a little niggle at the back of my mind; Brandon might be there. This could be my chance to show him what he's missing, prove I'm worth it.

'Lottie, Dad said dinner's ready,' my little sister says, as she barges into my room and scrunches her nose up at me in disgust. 'Euw, you really need to start learning how to contour or really just how to do makeup in general and stop wearing those lame skinny jeans,' she instructs, one hand on her hip and the other pointing at the sad case that is me. Her long curly blonde hair sits just above her waist and she blinks slowly with her beautiful long eyelashes and perfectly contoured face.

My eyes fall to her black long-sleeved crop top and perfectly toned stomach, her jeans are baggy and grungy looking. My sister really is beautiful and clever, which highlights my faults even more. She's also seventeen and a bit of a know-it-all unaffected by the unfairness of life yet. Call me cynical but she really doesn't know she's born yet. 'I'm thirty-one, that's how we old people roll,' I say, casually.

'No, that's what people ten years older than you do, you're still young enough to not be, she pauses to look me up and down. 'Totally bland and boring.'

'Cheers sis, you know how to kick a girl when she's feeling low, maybe I like being those things and maybe I don't care what's cool. It's cool not to care. You should try it sometime.'

Maggie's expression changes to a grimace and her lip gloss glistens next to her freshly bleached teeth, the teeth that really didn't even need bleaching in the first place.

'Okay, whatever. You're being weird now.' Maggie slams my door behind her as I lay there for a second considering my life choices. How did I end up back here arguing with my seventeen-year-old sister about how lame I look at the age of thirty-one?

'Hello Hammy,' Dad says, as I plonk myself down at the kitchen table. Yes, another nickname. Hammy is short for hamster as I used to have the world's largest cheeks. When I was a toddler people would often try and touch or pinch them, eventually I got fed up with this and would resort to biting them every time a finger came near me. In the end I only had to bare my teeth to keep the cheek pinchers at bay.

'Hey Dad, what's for dinner?'

'Beef bourguignon, I've been practicing,' Dad says, puffing out his chest and looking proud in his *I love baking* apron.

He's become a bit of a chef the last few years and has acquired skills galore as a stay-at-home dad. There isn't much to do in the way of hands-on parenting now that Maggie is older so he fills his days with renovating and decorating the house and garden and cooking up a storm in the kitchen. Mum's a lawyer and a very good one at that. She works on high interest cases that quite often involve celebrities and the unwanted attention from the media. She's feisty and smart whereas Dad is kind, funny and nurturing. An unlikely combination but one that has worked for many years. Mum says she never could have got with another lawyer, as she couldn't put up with someone as argumentative as her.

'Ooooh sounds fancy, where did you get this recipe from?'

'Out of that twerp's book, it's quite good.'

'Which twerp?'

'Oh, you know, the one who fancies himself a bit too much and can't say his r's.'

'Richard Ramsbury?'

'That's the one.'

'I think he's quite easy on the eye, Dad,' I tease, as Maggie pulls a face and Dad smirks before frowning.

'You can do better than the likes of him,' Dad says, waving his wooden spoon around as if he's casting a magic spell to banish all men. Please can he just banish the idiots.

'Dad, he wouldn't touch Hammy with a barge pole, he has a glittering career and a lovely family and Hammy has totally nothing going for her.'

'Cheers Sis, I do have nice hair and a glowing personality though,' I counter.

'Yes, you do my darling, yes you do and that's really all we need in life.' Dad beams before dancing back into the kitchen to tend to the beef.

'Yeah, if you don't want to sponge off your parents forever,' Maggie adds quietly as she eyeballs me. She really has it in for me today.

'I'm not sponging, I'm taking a life gap from all things responsible but I'll be back on track soon, levelling up. You'll see,' I say all matter-of-fact, feeling surprisingly upbeat about my secret plan to work on myself.

'Okkkaayyyy.' Maggie turns the corner of her lip up and goes back to her phone. It's sad the way we are now, there was a time when Maggie preferred me to our own parents but now, she appears to despise me. I'm everything she doesn't want to be, she resents me and that stings, just a bit.

'What are your plans this evening, Maggie?' Dad asks, as he walks back into the living room with our plates. The dinner smells delicious and for a second, I wonder if Mum and Dad would have me back indefinitely. But I'm not staying here long term, not even after the shock of Liam moving into Harry's. Harry apologised profusely for his forgetfulness, saying he agreed to Liam moving in absolutely ages ago then it completely exited his brain. He insisted that I stay on the sofa and not pay him a thing as he wants me to get on my own two feet asap. I considered it for a bit and decided that staying at Harry's would probably be better for my mental health. So there we are, after today, I'm moving back to Harry's again.

'Just going out,' Maggie replies, not looking up from her phone.

'Anywhere nice?' Dad asks.

'Just with friends.'

'Ahh friends, I remember those,' Dad says, as he begins to tuck into his dinner whilst eyeing her with a twinkle in his eye. I feel a pang of sympathy for Dad, he tries his best with Maggie but she's in full on teenager mode and just doesn't want to know. All she cares about is boys, makeup and Tiktok.

'I'm not doing anything tonight, Dad. We could watch

a film if you like?' I say. Dad's face lights up like a Christmas tree. He's the only one that will miss me when I move out.

'Really? That *would* be lovely, darling.'

'Cool, what do you fancy watching?'

'Well, I was going to say, that would be lovely but your Mum and I are otherwise engaged, we're going to a friend's house for drinks. It's her work friend so I have to make sure I swot up on all current affairs before I go.

'You don't need to do that, Dad, just be yourself.'

'If only it were that easy.' Dad smiles, then tucks into his dinner. He doesn't want to go.

'Sack them off, stay in with me. Mum won't mind,' I say, feeling suddenly emotional.

'Oh, she will. Anyway, you don't want to hang out with crusty old me, you're young. Go out! Seize the day.' He punches his arm up to the ceiling.

'She's not young,' Maggie says. We both ignore her.

'Okay, I might just watch *Stranger Things* then get an early night.' Both Maggie and Dad look at me with their mouths wide open and their eyes even wider.

'What? It's not that weird. This is the new me. No more going out every weekend. No more drinking to excess and leading Willow astray, we both agreed.'

'Yeah, we'll believe that when we see it,' Maggie says and Dad bites his lip in an attempt to stop himself from laughing.

They'll see. I won't be the laughing stock of the family forever. I've had a bit of bad luck and now it's time to stop feeling sorry for myself. Now it's time to re-focus on myself and get back my purpose and possibly my boyfriend.

Chapter 5

This morning I woke up in a glorious mood.

Ready for what the day brings, well rested and with a spring in my step. I hopped on the bus to work and smiled at everyone I made eye contact with. Now, that isn't too unusual in Coolsbay as we are quite a friendly community and we often say hello to each other, however this was different. I *properly* smiled at my fellow passengers. I mean my eyes smiled. I smiled and made conversations with them all, the old lady who always brings her big tartan trolley, the woman with the gurgling baby, the man with the ripped jeans and *Elvis* style hair, who normally never looks up from his newspaper. Just call me Miss Friendly Face, your casual happy woman about town. It was great until a woman told me to stop grinning like a lunatic at her boyfriend or she'd knock me out. Charming. Then I thought I'd better rein it in a bit. Not everyone knows or can appreciate my plan to level up as a person, especially those who aren't levelling up themselves.

'Wow, you're in a good mood today,' Willow chirps, as I bounce into the shop with my lunatic smile pasted back on again.

'Yes, yes I am. I've decided that's it,' I say, as I take

off my coat and hang it on the coat stand.

'What's what?' Willow appears from behind the cheese plant, looking a bit worried. 'You're not leaving, are you?' She looks genuinely concerned.

'No no, I'm not leaving yet but I do need to start applying for full-time job vacancies soon. Obviously I'll give you plenty of notice, Wills,' I say, as Willow nods in agreement. She knows this is only temporary; as much as we both enjoy it, it just isn't sustainable for either of us. 'Just no more feeling sorry for my sad life, it's time to level up.' I punch the air, as if that very action will propel me into the life I need, the life I know I deserve.

'Oh yes.' Willow claps her hands together. 'I love this! I'm so proud of you. Level up lady!'

'I knew I could count on you to be supportive.' I look around the shop in search of things to do. 'Where do you need me?'

'Ummmm well, you could clean those shelves over there and the window needs a bit of a reshuffle, maybe put together a bit of content for the *gram*?' she says, looking at me eagerly. If there's one thing I'm good at, it's content for the *gram*. Those few months jobless, sat around dabbling with social media in the day and when I couldn't sleep have seemingly given me a skill that not everyone has. Whenever I post a video of the shop people go a bit mad and we get a flurry of interest. Willow hates social media but she is slowly coming round to it since she's started reaping the benefits. 'The palms are a lot bigger than I anticipated but the umbrella plant could work quite well in the window. Oh, I'll be out this afternoon too, you okay to mind the shop until I get back?' Willow looks at me expectantly.

'Yes of course, doing anything nice?'

'Not really, but I shan't be long, couple of hours max.'

'Okay that's fiii…' I stop mid-sentence.

Willow widens her eyes at me and whispers, 'The Shmoo.'

Slowly, and as stealthily as possible, I turn my body towards the front shop window as Willow and I gawp at the man that we've nicknamed The Shmoo. He's on his own this time. His golden-brown wavy hair comes first as ever, bouncing in the wind in all its smoothness and gloriousness. This time he wears a chunky burgundy knitted scarf, speckled with black and grey. He runs a hand through his just-stepped-out-of-a-salon hair and Willow gasps. His feet, clad in navy-blue boat shoes, slap the pavement as his hips swagger underneath a thick green tweed jacket. He turns and gives us the most charming of smiles. Willow and I smile back, both giving a little wave before he disappears out of sight of the shop window and into someone else's fantasy.

'That man is just so beautiful,' Willow simpers, shaking her head. 'He seems so familiar too, but I just can't put my finger on it.'

'He is beautiful, but he absolutely knows it and he hasn't even been in your shop yet, the cheek of him,' I say. 'Especially as he only lives upstairs, it's only polite to pop in and say hi.'

'I know, but he will, just give it time,' she sighs. 'Do you think he has a girlfriend? A wife?' she asks, suddenly looking worried.

'I'm not sure, he definitely has some female friends but it's hard to tell. I've seen him with a toddler quite a few times too.'

'Have you?'

'Yeah, a little boy, about two years old.'

'Well, that doesn't put me off, I am forty, most men I meet now will be bound to have a little history.'

'Yeah, but there's history then there's another human in tow. Your son is all grown up, would you really want to do it all over again?'

'Oh, for The Shmoo I would.' Willow laughs but I'm not entirely sure she's joking. 'Maybe I could just rent him for a night or two, then I could go back to continuing to admire him from my window, like it never happened.'

'Willow! The poor man isn't an escort,' I snort, surprised at my friend's forwardness. She isn't normally this forthcoming about her thoughts towards men but today there seems to be something in the air and I'd be lying if I said I wasn't enjoying it.

'He'd make the perfect date though wouldn't he, to take to all those ghastly family events that you always dread going to because you're always on your own and everyone repeatedly pesters you about your love life, like it's up for discussion.' I nod in agreement, feeling her pain all too well as I'm reminded about the reunion email. I groan inwardly; I'm going to have to go it alone.

'He looks like he would yes, so how are we going to entice him in so you can get talking to him?'

'Well, I have a plan…'

Willow's plan wasn't what I expected. In fact, I don't know what I expected. All I know is that next week we're going to be loaning out a little corner of the plant shop to Missy Temple, the local crafting and interior design entrepreneur who sells knitwear including beautiful scarfs and you guessed it, boat shoes.

'But he already has loads of scarfs and his boat shoes look in pretty tiptop condition if you ask me.'

'Yes, but Missy also sells gorgeous wallets, gloves and plenty of other Shmooey things, that will be sure to entice him in.'

'And you don't think it will look a bit obvious that his entire wardrobe will be on show in the shop?' I snigger, as an image of The Shmoo running away with a terrified look on his face appears in my mind.

'No! There'll be women's stuff too of course; I won't make it look that obvious.'

'Well, I hope your plan works.'

'Me too, he's got to come in, I've been here for almost a year and I can tell he wants to, he's just looking for the right moment which I will now make easy for him.'

'You do make me laugh Willow.'

The next hour goes by quickly, Willow tending to the plants and me, cleaning and making videos and posts for social media. The doorbell jangles as Willow and I look up, turning on our full beam smiles for Malcolm the baker. He never buys anything but he always gives us the local gossip and occasionally the most delicious chocolate and peanut muffins from his bakery, just a few doors down.

'Ello ladies, how's it going?'

'Good thanks, Malc, and you?' Willow asks, as Malcolm's eyes twinkle.

'Yes, yes good, good can't complain.' Malcolm shuffles over, his little feet dragging on the floor and peeping out from underneath his huge white baker's jacket. 'Now, you didn't hear this from me,' he continues, lowering his voice. 'But a lady at Emmanuel's got the sack for bringing a fella into the shop in the middle of the night. She was caught in an entanglement in the changing rooms by non-other than Mr Emmanuel himself.'

'No way?' Willow and I squawk in unison.

'Uh huh. Also, there's rumours that Ravi has sold his shop to a woman who likes all them crystals and things.'

'Really? I can't believe he would just go without saying goodbye,' I say, before curiosity gets the better of me. 'A medium? Like a fortune teller?' I ask, as my stomach drops. I love Ravi and his little shop. He's been here for as long as I can remember, since before I was old enough to work. Willow gives me the side eye. It would not be good for my bank balance or my addictive personality if what Malcolm says is true. Which reminds me, I need to pay Ravi back. No, I don't need any of that anymore, I'm levelling up, without having my fortune told to me. I'm taking control and am going to make my future my own responsibility, not what a tarot card spread tells me.

'I'm not sure, but you didn't hear it from me, okay ladies.' Malcolm turns on his heel then twizzles back round again. 'Almost forgot, here you go.' He hands us a warm parcel, wrapped in brown paper. 'Let me know what you think, special recipe. Now, must go.'

Willow and I wait for him to leave before we open the delicious smelling parcel. The sweet smell of lemon hits my nostrils as I take a bite of the croissant and a gooey, creamy texture explodes in my mouth, satisfying all my senses.

'My God, this is better than sex,' I say to Willow, who nods in agreement.

'Don't let him hear you say that,' Willow says in-between stuffing her face and I laugh, giving her a gentle shove. 'He'll be back like a shot.'

'It's you he can't take his eyes off,' I reply, with a smirk.

'Shit, what's the time?'

'12 o'clock,' I say, after checking my watch.

'I'd better go or I'll be late, see you tomorrow,' she says stuffing the rest of the croissant into her mouth.

The next few hours drag; we anticipated January

would be quiet but today is another level. I get all of my jobs done then open up my laptop to begin my search for the new job which will eventually bring me financial freedom, freedom to buy my own place. As I scour the three recruitment agencies we have here in Coolsbay, I come across a couple of jobs that look okay but nothing that would push me out of my comfort zone. They are both PA jobs that pay fairly well, but one quite a bit more than the other. I apply for the one that pays the most because I deserve it. The old me would apply for the lower paid job because I would think I didn't deserve the higher paid job even though the job spec is basically the same. After getting bored applying for jobs that really don't excite me, I take more photos and videos of the plants before losing myself in promo videos and content planning for Aloe Lovely. By the time I've finished I've planned two weeks' worth of content and I'm very pleased with myself.

'Excuse me, do you have any philodendron plants?' A tall man in baggy colourful patchwork trousers and a *Mohawk* hairstyle asks, as I almost jump out of my skin. I don't know why he made me jump, it's not as if it's weird for people just to turn up, I do work in a shop after all. Despite the wacky attire, he's very attractive.

'Oh, umm, let me take a look, I think we may have a couple left.' I spring up from my seat as he watches me in amusement.

'Cool, I've been looking for one with particular shaped leaves, I'll know it when I see it.'

'Okay, let's hope we have the right leaves for you then.'

'How's this?' I hold up two philodendrons. One, in significantly better condition than the other, with its slightly brown leaves and a bit pathetic looking.

'Ahh perfect.' His face lights up and his olive-coloured eyes shimmer underneath the shop light. 'It's a bit broken, just what I was looking for, for my friend.' He reaches for the battered looking plant as his eyes meet mine.

'A guy can take much enjoyment in looking after things and watching how love can make them flourish,' he murmurs in a soft voice that makes me think of butter melting on hot toast.

'Yeah? That's wonderful,' I beam, blinking slowly as he gazes back at me.

Woah, where did he come from?

Chapter 6

Two weeks until the uni reunion and to get my life in check.

I'm really starting to panic now. I want to be able to stand proud against my peers as they talk about how life has been after uni and list their achievements but at the moment I just feel like the biggest loser aka victim. It's not my fault though, well not entirely.

Since receiving the uni reunion email, I've done sweet FA about getting my life on track apart from half-heartedly applying for a couple of full-time job positions and moving back to my parents then back to Harry's again.

Grabbing my phone from my bag, I check the time to see it's twelve pm. Saturdays are usually a work day but Willow insisted I have this one off as a thank you for increasing our sales and online presence. Kathy is keen for a housemate bonding session but I'm tired now and could have done with spending my day off in bed binging all the episodes of *Stranger Things* and eating all of the snacks I've just bought. It's too late to cancel now, plus I can't really escape, I live there, in the living room. To pass the time, I tap on the *Instagram* app and scroll past everyone performing and pretending they're living their best life for the *gram*. NextlevelNyssa is sat in a huge, beautiful bay window seat with big purple velvet cushions scattered around her. A big fluffy grey cat sits next to her. As always you can just see the back of Nyssa's shiny black bob as she hugs a mug of frothy steaming coffee and stares out onto a big manicured lawn. There are two trees to the left of the window with no leaves on as it's winter but hanging from them are beautiful wooden, coloured painted hearts. Underneath the photo she's written the caption.

NextlevelNyssa

Delve deep inside and focus on what you need, not what the naturally greedy self wants. We only need water yet many of us drink alcohol, abusing ourselves. We all know that alcohol isn't good for us, in fact it poisons the body, makes you think you're more confident than you actually are. True bravery is saying yes to water and saying yes to the stuff that scares yet excites you. The stuff that could enrich your life. In the words of Eleanor Roosevelt – 'do something that scares you every day.' What have you done today that has scared you?

Cut down on the booze. Tick. But I haven't done anything that scares me today, perhaps I should think of a career change. Go for something that scares me. But what would that be? My degree is in music so it's a pretty pointless degree unless you're ridiculously ambitious and know exactly what you want. I just played around with a few knobs and made some tracks that were actually quite awful. That degree really wasn't for me. What job would be good for me?

'Here she is,' Liam chirps, as he walks into the living room. He's all spruced up in a jumper and jeans. His thick beard looks neat and shiny, he must have oiled it or something.

'Oh, I forgot you were back,' I say which is true. He's

hardly been here since he supposedly moved in, always out working. Whenever I have seen him, he's been in grubby workman gear with mud or paint slopped all over him.

'Charming. Not just back, I'm living here, in your old room,' he goads. 'Living the dream and I'm also coming along today, isn't that nice and cosy, Grotty.' He folds his arms and grins a boyish grin that I'm sure many a girl has found hard to resist. But not me. To me he is too self-assured. He fancies himself way too much. A flash back of him in my training bra and all of my brother's mates laughing hysterically stings my memory. He was such a shit. I scowl at him.

'Great,' I say, smiling and frowning at the same time as I make eye contact with Kathy and she smiles a sympathetic smile.

'Hey Lottie,' Harry says, as I walk into the kitchen. 'Liam's booked for us to go on a party bike, isn't that great?' My brother grins then puts his arm around Liam, the golden boy. The golden gingerbread boy. His tan has faded slightly so he isn't so ginger looking now but he's still that lovely golden colour that fairish skinned people who tan tend to go. Despite being a quarter Italian with dark features, I burn like an angry blister in the sun.

'A party bike?'

'Yeah, it's a six-seater, my mate Beau actually made it from scratch, so impressive and it will be super fun, I promise,' Liam says.

'I'm not so sure about this,' Kathy pipes up with a wobbly voice and for once I agree with her. I don't think this is what she meant by housemate bonding.

'It will be grand, look we just wrap up warm, keep peddling and keep topping our beers up. What could be more fun?'

'Cheese and wine tasting down the Mermaid's Lair?' Kathy offers, and I nod despite feeling anxious about drinking.

'Come on guys! We aren't middle-aged quite yet, let's live a little,' Liam says, as Kathy and I exchange looks. I knew I should have stayed at my parents. 'Plus, it's my mate's new business so we'll be helping him out by giving him a good review.'

'What if it's awful?' I say.

'It won't be awful, Debbie downer,' he says, and I pull a face. 'It will be what you make of it, just like life.' His words hang in the air as Kathy and I reluctantly agree to go.

'Awww doesn't she look cute.' Liam laughs as I enter the room in Harry's enormous long winter coat, long scarf and big woolly hat. I look ridiculous. 'Like you're a little girl dressing up in her daddy's clothes.' He sniggers. Because I've been so indecisive and unorganised about where I want to live lately, I've left all my big coats at Mum and Dads. Liam said a denim jacket wasn't very clever, hence having to borrow Harry's stuff. Borrowing from Kathy was out of the question, she's a tiny size eight so I can't even fit my little finger into the arm of any of her coats. I scowl at Liam and shake the sleeves of the coat, already the itchy fabric lining of the coat is irritating my skin through my jumper. I glance over at my jacket and curse myself for not bringing my coats back. What was I thinking wearing a denim jacket in January?

'Well, I did think we'd just be sitting in a pub all day,' I say in my defence.

'You look *très chic*, Lottie,' Kathy says, putting her hand on my shoulder and smiling. I smile back. She badly wants us to get on and I should make more effort with my brother's girlfriend even if she is a little annoying. I've been a bit mean, all because I've been feeling down right miserable.

'Thanks babe, let's go and get fit and drunk!' I say, as I tap her hand and she beams back at me. I'd be lying if I said I wasn't looking forward to seeing Kathy drunk. NextLevelNyssa's previous post flashes in my mind's eye. I'll try and stay off the alcohol a little today, I've been really good recently, it would be a shame to spoil it now.

'Oh, I think they're here,' Harry says, looking out of the window. We all race over to see what this party bike thing looks like and it's quite the vison. It shakes violently as a huge comedy sized barrel of beer sits at the front of it. A couple sit on a bench behind the barrel as Beau turns the thin steering wheel, and the pedals move independently below three seats situated either side of a narrow table. It must have a motor somewhere because it's moving without the pedal power. It's painted a deep purple and has the words Beau's Banging Party bike emblazoned in gold across the thin rickety roof, which from looking at it, will just about cover our beers but not our backsides. This is going to be drafty. The bike comes to a grinding, shaky halt as it mounts the curb before the couple jump down from the driver's bench.

'Oh God, it looks like it could fall apart from us just looking at it,' Kathy whines, as Harry slings an arm around her to comfort her.

'It has got a roof though, so I'm ditching this coat, the wool is making me angry,' I say, as Harry and Liam exchange looks and I reach across to shrug my denim jacket back on. I don't need a big thick woolly coat, I'll be cycling and chugging beer for God's sake, that's enough to work up a sweat, let alone mere body heat.

We all stumble outside to meet Liam's mate who's come accompanied by a woman. They're both wearing black hoodies with the words Beau's Banging Party bike decorated across their chests in purple writing. The man, Beau, is jumping up and down doing some kind of weird dance until the woman, who's wearing a big bobble hat with meercats on, gives him a look and a tug on the arm which makes him promptly stop.

'Hey dudes, how's it going? How's the little one?' Liam says, gently squeezing the woman's shoulder before pulling the hyperactive Beau in for a hug. The rickety party bike stands behind the quirky couple and I vaguely wonder if they have a camper van decorated in the same fashion which they now call their home. They may even camp out on the party bike when it's warm.

'She's lovely thanks Liam, almost two now!' The woman says.

'Wow that's mental, guys,' Liam says, before he introduces us to his mates, Beau and girlfriend Laura. As we all stand there freezing, Liam explains he knows Beau from his stoner days when they both used to get their stash from Batshit Steve but now, thankfully, they've both turned their lives around.

'Wow, that's going way back, Batshit Steve, I didn't know he was still in the area,' Liam says, as Beau and Laura strap us into our seats and set up the beer.

'I heard he actually got time in the end, he tried to lay low during lockdown but he needed the cash so I think he was still out selling. I'm glad I found this out way after I quit or I may have been tempted to contact him and get my high on.' Beau nods quickly.

'So glad you didn't or we definitely *never* would have got together,' Laura remarks, making it clear who wears the trousers in this relationship.

'It was fate, babe. I gave up the crack for a great rack.' Beau points at Laura's boobs as she shakes her head and gives him a wry smile.

'He didn't give up crack guys, he's being facetious. I promise it was only weed but I do have a great rack, that bit's true,' she says, with a flick of the hair and we all agree as she moves herself towards the front of the bike, facing away from us.

'Right guys, let's get ready.' Beau raises his arm then sits next to me on one of the rickety seats. So now I'm sandwiched between the two crazies that are Beau and Liam. Kathy, who's sitting opposite me, catches my eye and grimaces. It has suddenly become bloody freezing.

'What do we do now?' Kathy squawks, her eyes so wide I can tell she isn't liking this already. Now she's clinging onto Harry's arm, blinking ferociously as if she thinks this thing is going to teleport us to another time zone. It would be cool if it did though, it can teleport me forwards in time to my new fulfilling, enriching life. If that's too greedy I'll take teleporting me to a date after the reunion when I'm back with Brandon.

My heart sinks.

But what if he's not there? Or worse, he doesn't want me back?

Beau levels his eyes with us and knits his fingers together; we all instinctively huddle in forwards and for a second, I get excited that he might say something profound or tell me the secret to being happy. I'm sure Liam mentioned something about him training to be a Reiki master, he's a very spiritual being, is how Liam put it. But no, here we go, I think as Beau raises a finger at Kathy and proceeds to talk, the health and safety talk. I think we all know there's nothing safe about drinking beer and cycling at the same time and yet this seems to be allowed to be a thing. God, please kill me, I'm starting to sound like Kathy.

'So how does it work?' Kathy says, sounding scared.

'Good question, Karen,' Beau says, nodding after the ten second health and safety talk which consisted of him telling us to just *not to be a dick and don't die* and you'll be okay. I could see Kathy's eyes becoming larger and larger the longer he spoke. I try to stop my eyes from rolling to the sky. Using the name Karen as an insult is so boring now, even my teenage sister has stopped using it.

'It's Kathy, mate,' Harry says for her with a frown and a shake of the head as Kathy smiles up at him. That's quite sweet, he's sticking up for her, her protector. I try to think of a time when Brandon did that for me, his parents were always interrogating me, always going on about why I wasn't using my degree and come to think of it, he never once told them to stop. That's what you need, someone who'll have your back and speak up when you're not being treated fairly but are too blind to see it for yourself. Oh, come on, he literally just corrected her name, what is wrong with me these days? I'm really missing having someone and my brother just reminded me of that. Yuck.

'Sorry, Kathy. Good question,' Beau says, then stands up with one hand on his heart and the other high up in the air. 'TODAY,' he bellows, pausing for dramatic effect before breathing in through his nose and then out through his mouth. He then lets out an almighty roar that makes us all jump. 'WE PEDAL AND WE POURRRRR.'

The roar really does excite everyone and we all scream then begin to pedal as fast as we can giggling with the absurdity of it all. The party bike moves surprisingly fast yet weirdly smoothly, perhaps it was the makeshift motor making it shake because peddling is quite easy and we don't have to worry too much because the much more sensible Laura is at the front of the bike steering it. Beau pours us frothy ale in thick pint glasses with handles and proceeds to tell us about the history of Coolsbay bitter before we pull up at a house made of old cobbled stones under a huge thatched roof. Beau tells us about the oldest house in Coolsbay and the first person to live in it. I'm enjoying learning more about my town, it's fascinating but I'm also bloody freezing.

'You alright there, Grotty?' Liam asks.

'It's Lottie and yes, fine thank you,' I say through gritted teeth, as I try to stop myself from shivering. It doesn't work and I begin to tremble even more, my legs and teeth marching to the beat of their own speedy drum. I chug my beer for more insulation then ask Beau for another, that will warm me up. Fuck levelling up. For now, I need to focus on keeping warm and staying alive.

Seconds later I feel something warm on my knee. That's nice, they've provided blankets, that's much better. Then I notice Liam take off his coat and try to sling it round my shoulders. Okay, who does he think he is?

'Umm no, no thank you, no need, I'm happy with the blankets they've provided.' I smile a tight-lipped smile then take a few more swigs of my beer. I would quite like to have something warm wrapped around my shoulders as it's still quite chilly despite the exercise but not from Mr (thinks he's a hero) Gingerbread Man, thank you very much.

'Well, you see that blanket on your knee.' He smirks. 'That's my scarf,' he says, leaving his teeth on his lips at the end of the word scarf. He's mocking me.

'Oh fancy that, I'm feeling much warmer now.' I drop

the scarf on his knees then inadvertently shudder.

'Don't be such a difficult woman.' He leans in and whispers so nobody else can hear and the hairs on the back of my neck betray me and stand on edge. Not that they're listening anyway as whilst this all goes on Beau has captivated everyone else with the tales of the Coolsbay sea monster. Legend has it that it surfaces once a year on the first of March, to check that everyone is treating each other with love and gratitude. 'I'm just trying to be nice, like the big sea monster wants me to,' Liam continues, placing a big warm hand on my thigh. He momentarily leaves it there for a matter of seconds and when he takes it away it leaves a big tingly handprint that travels all the way up my spine to my face. It must be the beer. I smile then look away. This time, I don't take the blanket scarf off.

'And if big old sea biscuit, I mean sea monster doesn't think that we, the people of Coolsbay, are treating each other nicely, speaking our truth, righting our wrongs, forgiving and forgetting those grudges,' Beau continues. 'He has a huge big paddy resulting in the heavens opening for the whole day and that's how we know we're in for a grim harvest for much of the spring and sometimes summer, that's if we've all been particularly *orrible* to each other.'

'So, he's basically not happy every year then? Because every year in March, April and May it thunders and rains.' Kathy titters, as my brother hugs her in a little closer.

'Well, my darling Karen,' Beau says, as my brother eyeballs him. 'I mean Kathy, sorry. I think the sea monster must be telling us something, don't you?'

'Yup, we're all miserable bastards that need to treat each other a bit better,' Harry pipes up and Beau nods and points at my brother.

'Yes, you sir have hit the nail on the head, let's just be nice.' Beau folds his arms behind his head.

'IT'S NICE TO BE NICE,' Laura shouts from the front of the bike before signalling to Beau to bring out the bowls of crisps, nuts and chocolates. My cheeks tingle matching the slight burn in my thighs from all the peddling. This is an odd experience but a really fun one so far.

'Let's try and make this year different then, let's all just be a bit kinder to one another and pray for a nice mild day on the first of March,' Kathy says, as her eyes rest on me and I feel a glimmer of guilt. Kathy's not so bad, she's just making an effort with her boyfriend's sister. Who cares if she loves dollies? It doesn't make her a bad person, just a bit of an odd one and aren't we all a bit odd in our own way?

Beau pours everyone a shot of something pink and sticky and we all say cheers to that.

'Woah, this stuff is potent.' Liam coughs then looks at me. His eyes are blood shot. I laugh before grabbing a handful of nuts, I gobble them down then without taking my eyes off him I down another pink sticky shot.

I'm so cool.

Not.

I'm really not cool.

I grab onto Liam's wrist and cough and splutter like a ninety-year-old who smokes fifty cigarettes a day.

'Yeah, yeah, very funny. I don't think I looked quite that bad,' Liam jokes, as the rest of the gang laugh at something Beau's said about Coolsbay being the first beach in the UK to hold a week-long nudist festival in the eighties.

Meanwhile, I'm still choking.

I can't breathe.

'OH FUCK,' Liam bursts out, as realisation sets in that I could actually be struggling to breathe at this point. 'Stop the bike. Stop the fucking bike wagon thing, she's choking,' he shouts, as the party bike comes to a jolty halt and I feel strong arms around my waist.

'Okay, one, two, three,' Liam says, before he throws me around, thrusting forcefully over and over again until the stubborn little nut dislodges itself from my throat. It knocks the wind out of me and the nut right out of my mouth and straight into Kathy's eye. There's a brief sigh of relief that I'm still alive before the screams come from Kathy.

'Mate, where did you find these birds? They're a fucking liability,' Beau laughs, then promptly stops as the screams coming from Kathy go up an octave. It was a spicy nut, not good to choke on but especially not good if it ends up in one's eye.

One warm compress and two very bruised, potentially fractured ribs later and Kathy and I are doing alright, spread out on the sofa at my brother's house. We could have taken a trip up A & E but luckily Laura, Beau's girlfriend, is a trained nurse so she tended to our injuries whilst Beau tried to keep everyone jolly with more tales of Coolsbay History.

'Thanks for saving my life,' I say to Liam, in an attempt to sound grateful and thankful but it comes out high pitched and whiny. He looks at me, grins then winks, then places a hand on my back.

'That's okay, next time you have to return the favour though.'

'Yeah, but I'll try and fracture an extra rib just for good measure,' I quip, as he removes his hand from my back and slides it down his leg. I hold my breath which hurts my ribs.

'Oooh you're mean, it was potentially fractured ribs or die choking.'

'I know. Thanks,' I say, and I mean it although I hate that it had to be him who saved my life.

'And how are you feeling Kathy? Did your dreams really come true yet?'

'What dreams?' Kathy asks innocently, as Liam begins humming a tune and Harry and I try not to burst out laughing, it's singer Gabrielle's *Dreams*. My mum and dad used to play it all the time when we were growing up, I always thought she looked so glam with all of her different fancy eye patches, and hearing it makes me want to decorate Kathy's patch.

'Come here baby, I like a sexy pirate,' my brother murmurs in Kathy's ear, as Liam pretends to stick his fingers down his throat. I press my lips together to hold in a giggle.

My phone beeps and I reach into my pocket to see who it is.

Willow: *Hello babe, please feel free to say no but I have a favour to ask. Would you mind the shop for a week, maybe a little longer? I have to take some last-minute leave, family emergency. Mum's actually quite ill and Dad needs a bit of help. They've been trying to hide it from me. Naughty parents. xx*

Seconds later there's another text from Willow. She almost always texts twice.

Willow: *It's so cheeky of me I know but I don't know anyone else who can do it. Is that alright? P.S I'm fine, don't worry. Love you xxx*

'Oh shit,' I say out loud and everyone looks at me. 'Willow wants me to look after the shop, for a week. On my own.'

Do one thing every day that scares you. I quickly type my reply, NextlevelNyssa would be proud, I've done plenty of scary things today.

Me: *Yes of course, I'm so sorry about your mum mate but what are friends for? Your shop is safe with me.*

Famous last words.

Chapter 7

Right. Here goes. My first day as the boss for a week.

It can't be that hard running a shop, can it? I step on the bus and tap my card to pay.

'Oh 'ello love, you're early, what's up?' Rupert the bus driver, who must be pushing eighty but is always so sweet and cheery leans forward then lowers his voice. 'Did you shit the bed? It can happen to the best of us, I should know.' He winks then shakes his head.

'No, Rupert.' I laugh then flick my unruly hair back, someone behind me shouts ouch and I quickly apologise before turning back to Rupert.

'Today, well this week I have the big responsibility of running Aloe Lovely all on my own, so I'm going in extra early to make sure I'm organised and set for the day.

'Good for you, you'll smash it, as the young folk like to say these days.'

I thank him then find my favourite window seat. I'm also going in extra early to finally pay Ravi back, it's been weeks since I've stepped foot in the corner shop. I'm curious to see if Malcolm's gossip is true and ask him if he really has sold it. Ravi's opens at six am so he'll definitely be open by the time I get there at seven am. The plant shop doesn't actually open until ten am but I want everything to run smoothly in Willow's absence; she said she's left me instructions but I want to make sure I follow everything to a tee. I want to do my mate proud, especially as she must be under a lot of stress with her mum being ill.

The sun rises over Coolsbay as we enter the town centre. It's so peaceful this time of morning; Coolsbay doesn't really get going until ten am, especially in the winter. It's a slower pace of life here. For many, January is a sad depressing month, but for me this time I'm seeing it as a chance to reflect, rest and generally be peaceful. That's what my new life guru NextlevelNyssa suggests you do anyway. Oh God, listen to me! Brandon would have laughed his head off but then he was a big dickhead as Liam would say. I let out a little giggle and shake my head as an image of Liam giving me the Heimlich manoeuvre comes to mind coupled with Kathy screaming at her eyeball of fire. What a fucking mess the end of the night turned out to be, that party bike was a good laugh though, except I very much doubt Liam is ever going to let it drop that *he* saved my life. My giggle turns to an inward groan as I reach my stop. Just a few more months and I can whack out the roller skates, I can't wait for that, much healthier and free too. *Or maybe you could get a car?* A little voice niggles at the back of my mind. Like a real grown up.

I get off the bus and make my way down the high street, everything is closed but I'm certain Ravi's will be open. As I approach the shop though, something looks off. In fact, the more I look at the shop the more I have to double check my surroundings to make sure that I'm at the right place. Of course, I am, it's just that Ravi's isn't Ravi's anymore. It's now named Estelle's Crystals and everything is pink, gold and purple. The shop door has even changed, what was once a dark green modest door that was always open, is now a gold, grand door with a lion for a doorknob. I peer through the window, half expecting to see Scrooge and Tiny Tim sitting at their desks working away. Instead, the room is almost bare with freshly painted pale pink walls, and just a few crystals, of all different shapes and sizes, dotted about on circular-shaped shelves. My eyes are drawn to a black curtain to the back left of the room.

'Sorry I'm not open yet, but you can book an appointment if you like,' a raspy voice says, as I inadvertently jump back from the shop door and almost step on this woman's, or should I say girl's, toes. She's small, smaller than me and has her hair scooped up in a high ponytail. Her eyes are outlined with perfect flicks and lashings of black mascara.

'Oh right, sorry, I was looking for Ravi, I have something for him that's all.'

'The guy that owned the shop before me?'

'Umm yeah.'

'Ahh okay, I can see if I can get his details for you if you like, come on in.' She waves me in with a big welcoming smile, then takes off her floor length coat. She's dressed in a beautiful A-line patchwork dress and wears three necklaces around her long neck, each one bearing a different stone.

'Okay.' I step inside the shop as the girl slides behind the counter and starts to sift through countless trays. Not satisfied, she switches on the laptop and begins to tap away until she claps her hands together.

'Got it! His email. I knew it was here somewhere. I'll write it down for you.' She scribbles it down on a scrap of paper and hands it to me.

'Thanks so much, that's really helpful of you,' I say

and smile at her.

'No problem,' she replies as my eyes travel around the shop again.

'Do you know why he left so suddenly?'

'Oh, he didn't, he sold the shop ages ago but I don't think he wanted anyone to know.' She bites her lip and I wince inwardly, feeling guilty that I didn't get to pay him back or say goodbye. It's all very sudden.

'Ahh right, and you don't know where he's gone?'

'I don't, sorry.'

'No worries.' I smile. 'Thanks for your help.'

'It's not a problem at all,' she says as she holds up a sign that says, *Free tarot. Today only.* A gasp escapes me as she catches me staring at it. She smiles knowingly. 'Fancy a free reading?' She says in a bubbly loud tone as she confidently studies me. 'I'm only doing it today as it will be my first full day open.'

'Totally free?' I double check.

'Totally free.' She nods quickly then laughs at my gobsmacked face.

'Yes please, sign me up,' my mouth says before I can stop it. Oh shit.

Five minutes later and I'm booked in for a tarot reading after the shop's closed and I can't bloody wait. What are the chances of having this place right on my doorstep? Just one free reading won't hurt. I arrive at the plant shop to find a list on the counter of stuff that Willow wants me to get done, it isn't much and I can tell she's being easy on me. After I've watered the plants that need watering and added new plants to the website. I rearrange a few things in the shop then film a few videos to upload to social media. January is always quiet so there should be a bit of time to take photos and market this place. I want to do Willow proud. I know she doesn't like asking for the marketing help as she feels she should pay me more.

The first few hours whizz by and by the time it's opening time, there's a little queue of people waiting outside to get in. I thought January was supposed to be quiet; not so, today. I spend the next hour and a half running around fetching plants and apart from the odd sly Google search when no one is looking I surprise myself with my knowledge and customer service. The shop becomes quiet again after the little flurry of customers so I flick on the kettle to make myself a well-deserved cup of coffee and a cheeky pickled gherkin. No sooner has my bum hit the seat then the doorbell jangles and in trots Missy Temple carrying a rather large cardboard box.

'I'm after Willow,' she says, with a swish of her hair as the cold follows in after her and she sets the box down next to her feet. She is very well put together in tight dark denim jeans, expensive looking knee-high boots, a crisp pale blue shirt and an undone quilted jacket. Her makeup is immaculate and her blonde bob sits perfectly just above her shoulders. She shakes her head slightly, stomps her foot and I brace myself for a little neigh or snort that never comes. She's so glam. I bet anyone would feel shabby by comparison.

'I'm afraid Willow isn't here this week,' I say slowly. Shit, I can already tell this isn't going to go down well.

'Not here?' She scoffs.

'No, can I try and help at all?' I try not to cower in her scary presence. Missy looks me up and down, deciding if I'm worthy enough to help her. She narrows her eyes then shakes her hair again and stomps her foot. Again, the neigh doesn't come.

'I'm supposed to have my pop-up shop in here from

tomorrow and I wanted to chat with Willow about where I can put everything. Can you do that?' she asks me, with a twizzle of her finger.

'I can certainly try, lovely boots by the way.' I smile and Missy's lip twitches slightly. Was that a smile?

'I hope you *can* help,' she says, looking at me pointedly. 'Right which corner's mine?' she asks, as my eyes scan the shop floor to see which corner would do best.

'What about here?' I say, pointing to the left corner of the shop. She looks at me blankly then swivels her head to the left and then to the right as if checking to see who's listening.

'Are you stupid?' she hisses, and I look around to see if anyone else heard that but it's just us in the shop. Perhaps I misheard.

'Sorry?'

'Are you stupid?' she repeats. 'The customers will walk straight past my stock; nothing will get seen. Next suggestion please.' She folds her arms together and begins tapping her foot impatiently. I really want to tell her to do one right now but this is Willow's shop so I suck it up and smile sweetly.

'Okay, well how about this corner, your stock will be the first thing that the customers see,' I suggest. She looks even less impressed.

'Are you stupid?' she asks again and my mouth falls open.

'She's not stupid at all but I'd be stupid to pay these prices for a flimsy looking scarf,' a buttery sounding male voice says as Missy stares at Mohawk Man like a rabbit caught in headlights.

'Oh hello, we do them in a thicker knit too,' she says, in a much more pleasant tone. 'I have a burgundy one

64

which would totally suit your colouring and style, Mr Woodling.' She smiles a pretty smile that would totally win me over if she hadn't just been a complete bitch and called me stupid.

'No need for the formalities,' he says, with a wave of his hand. 'And none of this is my style anyway. Bit too high street for me, I prefer much more modest clothes, second hand or made by lovely sincere people. Do you know what I mean?' he asks Missy as she continues to smile like she's auditioning to be a beauty queen. She's lost for words and I press my lips together to stop myself from laughing. Mohawk Man has quite the authority over her. Who is this quirky, manly stranger?

'Of course,' she simpers. 'We can't please everyone.'

'No, but we can try to be pleasant to everyone, say sorry to my friend please.' Oh my God.

'Sorry ummm…' Missy shuffles on her feet from side to side.

'Lottie,' I say sweetly and Mr Woodling winks at me.

'Sorry, Lottie,' Missy says, looking at her feet.

'Right, that's better,' he says to Missy, as she stands there like a naughty told off child. 'I'll call you later about the restaurant,' he says in a kinder voice. 'We need to get the ball rolling now with the interior design. 'Have you booked the painters?'

'Yes, just the one guy but he's very good.'

'Okay, fine. That reminds me, Lottie, I came in to tell you that philodendron was a hit, it's positively flourishing, do you have any dragon trees?' I spend the next fifteen minutes fussing over Mr Woodling as Missy stands around looking awkward. Once he's gone, Missy is still a little off which is to be expected as she has had her nose put out of joint but she is polite and much more cooperative. After much deliberation we settle on the original spot for her pop-up shop. Missy concludes that low and behold it does actually have the best lighting. I pop her box behind the desk and let out a big sigh. It was nice to have a stranger stick up for me, but not only that, he's quite easy on the eye, too.

Chapter 8

Hi Ravi,

It's Lottie from Aloe Lovely, I hope you don't mind but I got your email address from the lady who's taken over your shop space. I wanted to see how I can pay back the money you so kindly lent to me a few weeks ago? Anyway, hope to hear from you soon and I hope you're doing well in your new venture whatever that may be. Hope you and your family are well? You are very much missed here on the Coolsbay high street.

Lottie

I tap send then scroll on my phone before ending up at my favourite corner of the internet.

NextlevelNyssa

The answers are always within you but to hear them you have to be able to drown out that exterior noise. Take a moment to listen to yourself. Be quiet. What is your intuition saying? Truly connect to your instincts – you have all the answers within you, I promise.

I gaze at the photo of Nyssa meditating, as always you can only see the back of her. She's wearing a lose two-piece black gym set and is sitting crossed-legged on white painted decking. She looks out towards the sea and the sun is just peeping out over the horizon. She must have got up bloody early for that but it looks like heaven.

Nyssa seems to have all the answers. I scroll down and read the comments from all of her followers ranging from worship to scepticism, it appears even Nyssa can't win them all but does she care? Probably not. Maybe I should try meditating. Maybe, but right now I'll settle for a free tarot card reading, that will do nicely.

I pad down to Estelle's Crystals and reflect on my first day looking after the shop by myself and give myself a big pat on the back. Willow's list was completed and more and I managed to keep my mouth shut and keep my cool when Missy Temple called me stupid. It's all in a hard day's work and this is my treat.

'Hello again,' the girl sings, as I push open the door and walk over to the desk. Dionne Warwick's *Say a little Prayer* is playing in the background and I smile, it briefly reminds me of my dad, he loves a bit of Motown.

'Hi, I'm here for the free reading,' I chirp a little too cheerily.

'I remember. I connected to your energy earlier, we've got some work to do.'

'Oh,' I say, not knowing what else to say and wondering if I'm exuding big dick energy yet.

'Sorry, that must have sounded a bit much if you're not used to it,' she says with a giggle, as she locks the door. 'But it's all good, come this way.' I follow her to the black curtain; she sweeps it aside to reveal a tiny room with a small wooden table and two chairs with pink cushions. A tall lamp stands in the corner, watching and potentially judging me. On the table are a pack of tarot cards. We sit down opposite each other and she takes the pack of cards and begins to shuffle.

'Simple spread, past, present and future,' she says and I nod in agreement.

'Of course, it's free, I'm happy with whatever.'

She smiles and passes the cards to me, instructing me to split them into three piles and face them upwards, I do as I'm told then stare down at the three cards.

'I've got the death card,' I say flatly, as beads of sweat begin to form on my forehead. From all of the tarot readings I've had online, I've never had that card before. It surely can't be a good thing. I swallow the saliva that's gathered in my mouth and brace myself for the bad news that I'm probably going to die tomorrow a sad and desperate young woman with droopy boob energy.

'That's your present,' she says. I frown thinking that death isn't much of a gift, 'But first, let's focus on your past.' She points to an upside down Two of Cups card and I nod, feeling relatively calm about my impending doom.

'I see a breakup, not too long ago.' She looks at me to gauge my reaction and I nod with a straight face. 'He took from you,' she says with her eyes closed. 'Yes, he took too much.' Yup, my home for one. 'There was an imbalance in the relationship, you should have asked for more but now it's done. Don't be afraid.'

She opens her eyes and I press my lips together, why do I feel so emotional all of a sudden? This is ridiculous. The online readings never did this.

She swiftly puts her hand up, making me jump before she slaps it down on top of my hand. 'STOP thinking about what you've lost and focus on what you have. He needed to go, he needed to explore and you, you have what you need right here.' She taps on the table with her long, dark purple finger nails and I fight the urge to groan. I wish everybody would just tell me what's inside me that I already have, because apart from way too many pickled gherkins, I honestly don't have a clue. The girl moves her finger to the death card and I let out a little gasp.

'Don't worry,' she grins wildly. 'This card is good. The best in fact. You're going through some changes right now; everything is happening for the greater good. Things will start to shift soon.' I feel my nose scrunch up, suddenly sceptical at the plethora of clichés coming from her mouth. The girl makes strong eye contact with me and lowers her voice. Something in her expression shifts and her eyes darken. 'The reunion is coming and the escort will bear a scar on his jaw. Pay attention to the escort,' she continues, as she taps on the table. I gasp as she turns over the final card and reveals, The Lovers. 'The laughs will be plenty and new love is challenging but just around the corner for you.'

I leave the shop with the girl's words ringing in my ears, what does she mean? A scar on his jaw? An escort? Brandon doesn't have a scar on his jaw, but he may do now after all his travelling. My mind wanders to his most recent blog post about the crocodile in Australia. Perhaps moments later, he fought said crocodile off and now dons a scar, who knows? The only person I want to talk to this about this, is Willow.

Me: *Ravi's has gone! I'll explain when you're back. We now have a crystal shop that does tarot readings. Just had a tarot reading and she said that the one who escorts me to the reunion shall have a scar on his jaw. I wasn't planning on bringing anyone but now I feel like I should? But who? Mr Woodling seems nice but it would be so weird to ask him as I barely know him. P.S shop's good – don't worry. Hope your mum is okay. xx*

Minutes later when I'm on the bus on my way home, my phone pings.

Willow: *What the fucculent? I thought you weren't doing those bloody things anymore! But this has come as a most welcome distraction. She's telling you to hire a bloody escort, honestly, it's plain as day. I dare you. I love you. This could be the modern-day Pretty Woman we've all been waiting for.* I wait for the imminent next message.

Willow: *Thank you for everything, really appreciate you holding the fort. Mum is getting better, should be back next week. Xx*

Me: *That's great news about your, mum. It was free! I'll explain when you get back. An escort? Oh God, no way! xx*

Willow: *If the Shmoo turns up as your escort then send him to me immediately. Xx*

Me: *I'm not booking a bloody escort.* Xx

Willow: *Do it. You only live once.*

Me: *No. Kindly fucculent off. xx*

Quietly, I chuckle to myself at Willow's paranoia of The Shmoo being an escort. Her brain has turned to Shmoo. Seconds later Willow sends me a link to a local escort agency that specialises in women's dating services. She sent that way too fast. I feel a smirk spread across my lips, wondering if she's already used their services herself. Willow and her ex-husband did like to frequent the adult night clubs from time to time so anything is possible. But an escort? The tarot card reader couldn't have meant that, surely?

I can't take an escort to my university reunion.

Where my ex might be.

No way.

It can't happen.

Chapter 9

If Brandon attended the reunion and saw me with somebody else, it might make him insanely jealous and fall back in love with me. She did say love was just around the corner… this might not be as ludicrous as it first sounded. It might take this for him to realise what he's lost. Desperate times call for desperate measures.

Creeping into the living room/my bedroom, I call out everyone's name thinking that Kathy might be asleep with a doily on her face on her sofa/my bed. When I'm satisfied that no one is actually home yet and I have the house to myself, I do a little dance around the living room. It's odd that no one is home yet but I'm certainly not complaining and this leaves me with the freedom and peace to work up the guts to book my date or should I say, my escort. Escort sounds so seedy, doesn't it? Let's just stick with date. Flumping down on the sofa I shriek into the cushions in a new haze of hysteria, this is ridiculous but what else could the tarot reader have meant? I'm excited. It's destined. Calm down Lottie! Who knows this *date* could be the one to make my ex jealous and want me back again. But will I even want him back when I see him again? Knowing me, probably.

I spend the next half an hour scrolling various profiles

until I stumble across someone that catches my eye. He's about my age, maybe slightly older, with dark hair and eyes. His smouldering looks pull me in before I become lost in his witty and charming profile. This guy, who goes by the name of Ed or Eddie, has many shining reviews. I click on every single one, each one a five-star, complimenting Ed on his professionalism and discreet nature. He charges by the hour, so not that cheap. But it will be worthwhile to dip into my savings for this and for a first time booking they do offer a twenty-five percent discount. I do the maths and realise it will be best to book him for twenty-four hours. There must be a reason it's called, *No kisses male escort agency*. Holding my breath, I fill out the forms and send them over. Minutes later, my phone pings through with the confirmation. Shit. I'm really doing this. I've truly lost my mind. With shaking hands, I send a message to Willow.

Me: *I've just booked an escort for my reunion. This is fucking mental. I'm petrified and it's partly your fault. Hahaha.*

Willow: *Oh my god you did it! That's amazing. I can't wait to hear all about it. What an adventure. Aiming to be back Thursday. Love you xx*

Me: *Love you too, hope your mum's okay. Xxx*

Willow: *She's getting there and thank you. Did Missy show up by the way? How does the pop-up look?*

Me: *She's setting it up tomorrow, came in today to get her bearings. It's going to look fab, the Shmoo will be running through the doors in no time. Xx*

I don't tell Willow about Missy being a complete bitch as I don't want to upset her and make her worry, at least Missy will just be setting up and then going away. It's a pop up, so we don't require the business owner to hang about and Willow has made that perfectly clear, thank God.

The front door slams making me jump and I frantically tap to get out of my escort booking before anyone sees. The delicious smell of fish and chips infiltrates my nostrils, shortly followed by excited chatter and a blast of fresh, frosty air. So that's where they've been, getting tonight's dinner. My stomach growls, sounding like an angry bear. In the busyness and excitement of today, I realise I haven't eaten a thing all day apart from a couple of pickled gherkins from the jar that I keep in the fridge at work. It's a silent addiction as well as a bit of a stinky one which is why I always carry plenty of chewing gum with me. I know that I should tame it down if I want to win Brandon back, he was always grossed out by my odd habit, especially when he caught me dipping them in lashings of sour cream, straight out of the pot. Absolute pure bliss pickled heaven.

It could be worse; I could be addicted to crack or escorts.

'Hey sis, couldn't get you any pickled gherkins so got you a pickled egg to go with,' my brother says, as the smell of chips and fresh air make me giddy. I am bloody starving.

'Ah close but no cigar Hazza, but I guess that will have to do,' I joke, as everyone piles the brown paper-wrapped packages of food onto the table and Kathy scurries off to the kitchen. I follow after her to help sort out drinks but Liam, it appears, has beaten me to it. I make myself useful scrambling around in the fridge for the condiments.

'Glass of wine?' he asks, with a raised eyebrow, as he watches me pour myself a squash. Just because he's saved my life it doesn't mean we're friends. He *has* stolen my bedroom, after all.

'No thanks, I've got work tomorrow and I need to be on the ball,' I reply with a breezy smile, feeling slightly smug at the new sensible me. Apart from the night on the party bike which left me feeling groggy and depressed the next day, I haven't drunk at all in months and I'm enjoying having a clear head too much.

'Okay,' he says raising his eyebrows and nodding slowly. 'Kathy?'

'Oh, go on then,' she says, massaging her own neck. 'It's been one shit of a day.' I almost spit my squash out. Kathy NEVER swears.

'What's happened?' I ask, as Liam catches my eye. Poor Kathy.

'Urgh, just one thing after another. A negative spiral is what I call it,' she says as I feel myself relate to her words on so many levels. 'The day started bad and just got worse and now I need to drink to forget. Forgive me whilst I behave like a wild woman tonight.' She bends down and gets out the plates.

'Now this I'd like to see.' Liam chuckles as I dig him in the ribs.

'Go wild, Kathy, let it all out. What are housemates for, after all?' I know how things can spiral quickly out of control.

'Thanks guys.' She rearranges her eyepatch which she's painted (after my suggestion) a freaky bright blue eye on that stares at you in a very accusing manner. She picks up the plates and cutlery. 'I just want to have a good laugh, you know?' she says, as her freaky eye patch glares at me.

We walk back into the living room and tuck into our fish and chips in silence.

'Okay, pumpkin?' Harry says to Kathy. She nods with a full mouth then gives him the thumbs up.

'God I've missed this, they don't do fish and chips like this in Thailand,' Liam says.

I notice he's dressed in really scruffy clothes and has what looks like flicks of paint on his t-shirt and face. An image of him going up and down a ladder carrying heavy tins of paint and flexing his biceps springs into my mind. The corners of his mouth twitch and I realise I've been day dreaming, staring at his arms. Oh shit.

'What was it like out there?' I ask, half curiosity getting the better of me and half wanting to project any attention away from my wandering eye. Kathy's accusing eye patch stares at me again. She caught me staring too. His eyes light up when he talks of his travels and the projects that people are putting in place for the next trip. A wave of what I can only call respect washes over me as he shows compassion for the disadvantaged teens' stories. He did a good thing. Many good things. He may be a bit of a dickhead but he went out there and helped and what's more he actually enjoyed it and wants to do it again. I tilt my head and slyly study him, watching for any signs of insincerity or boastfulness. Either he's really good at pretending he's a decent person or he's actually turned into one.

The jury is still out on that one.

After a late night playing Coolsbay limited edition Monopoly and stopping Kathy from drowning her sorrows in too many shots of neat whiskey because she had a run in with a rude customer who said they were going to report her to head office, the next day rolls around quickly. I wake up dribbling to the smell of bacon coupled with the sound of not so quiet singing. It could only be Liam with that deep Irish lilt. Well, it's much better than listening to my brother and Kathy's loud sex screams. I could get used to the sofa life. After her fourth shot last night, Kathy admitted that she was cross at Harry for letting what she thought was his slobby sister sleep on their brand-new sofa but now she's got to know me a bit better and seen how lovely I am, she's doesn't mind so much anymore. She then proceeded to put a doily on each boob and dance around the living room like Madonna. Kathy has definitely gone up in my estimation.

I indulge myself in a big stretch and yawn on the comfy sofa then listen intently as Liam sings something about horses and about *never being able to go with you no matter how he wanted to*. He can hold a tune no doubt, but it's seven am in the bloody morning, way too early for so much noise. Anyone who knows me, knows I value my sleep and unless I've had time to mentally prepare for it and it's on my terms, I need my seven – eight hours. Any less and I'm a raging monster. I have work, but not until ten o'clock so I would have gotten up at eight at the absolute earliest. What the hell is he playing at? I listen for a few more seconds as the volume of singing gets even louder as he belts out about riding the finest horse. As the singing dramatics increase so does the clattering of plates and cutlery. Not being able to take anymore, I stomp into the kitchen and am met with a half-naked jolly Liam singing about riding the finest horse.

'Jesus Christ, Joseph, Mary and the little donkey she rode in on, you half scared me to death,' he says, as he turns round to find me standing in the kitchen doorway, arms folded across my oversized checked pyjamas. I raise an eyebrow at him and tilt my head, hoping he gets the message without me having to open my mouth. 'You

kinda look like a mega scary medusa with all that hair.'
He laughs, pointing at my hair that's piled high on top of
my head.

'It's called a pineapple, it keeps my hair in place so I
don't have to do much to it in the morning,' I reply. He
stares at me like I have two heads. 'For curly hair. We do
things differently.' I explain with a wave of my hand.

'You best not be going out like that, you'll give people
an awful fright. It's quite an impressive structure though,
it must increase your height by at least a foot.' He reaches
over to touch my hair and I bat his hand away, then
swiftly fold my arms again, suddenly self-conscious that
I'm not wearing a bra.

'Do you have to get up so early and make such a
bloody racket singing about horses at the top of your
lungs?' I growl, folding my arms tighter to my chest. He
leans over to touch my hair again but my glare makes him
think twice about it.

Do not touch me, the last time you did felt weird.
Weirdly nice.

'It depends. Do you have to be such a grumpy old
Grotty?' He laughs again then turns back to his bacon
before resuming the horse song.

I huff then turn on my heel back to my
bedroom/living room to sort out my outfit for today. I
decide on my dark purple dungarees with daisies on and
a long-sleeved green t-shirt. I love being able to wear
what I want to work; when I was a PA I had to dress in
smart office attire at all times, it felt stuffy and just not
me. My stomach drops, I wonder how long it will be until
I have to wear those clothes again. I make a mental note
to chase up the jobs I've applied for. Minutes later Liam
strolls into my bedroom/living room carrying a tray with
two plates and two mugs.

'Nice knickers,' he comments, as his eyes fall to my laid-out clothes. Yes, I'm matching my daisy dungarees with some huge, comfy knickers with a big daisy on the front.

'Keep your eyes off my flower,' I blurt out and we both burst out laughing. The mood instantly lifted.

'I made you a bacon sandwich, to say sorry for being a loud gobshite.' He holds the tray out to me and I reluctantly take a plate. I look up at him and he nods down at the cup of tea so I take that too, then quickly avoid further eye contact. He has those type of eyes that look at you too much, if you know what I mean. They make me feel too seen. Maybe that's why some blue eyes are called piercing because that's what they do, pierce into your thoughts, your soul even.

It's too early for soul piercing.

'Thank you,' I manage, then busy myself with eating my bacon sandwich. Liam sits himself down in the armchair and flicks on the TV, he settles on the news or rather what I like to call the *bad* news.

'Doesn't all this depress you?' I say, after listening to the solemn headlines of a murder, a robbery and the global climate change crisis.

'A bit, I guess.' He shrugs then goes back to watching it for a few minutes as the news goes into gruesome detail about the murder. 'But it's better to be in the know than be ignorant, don't you think?' he says without looking at me, then takes a bite of his sandwich.

'Oh, I don't know, sometimes it's nice to be ignorant, rather that sometimes than pollute my mind with all the bad news, it's always so negative,' I say, then watch him whilst taking a sip of tea.

'You know that sounds not only ignorant but arrogant too.' It isn't what he says but the sing songy voice that he says it in. It's the same tone he used to tease me with when we were younger. I glare at him as he looks at me with his intruding eyes and, I feel my blood begin to boil. He's touched a nerve, to say the least.

'Does it now? And you would know all about that, wouldn't you? Mr I'm so worldly and wise.' I put my sandwich down as he stares at me with his mouth open. 'You need to give your head a good wobble so all of those pretentious pearls of wisdom fall out of your ears and you can hear that others have different opinions to you,' I say, feeling like a hormonal teenager. I pick my clothes up and stomp out of the living room to go to the bathroom to get dressed.

I hate not having a bloody room.

I hate sharing everything with *him*.

Chapter 10

Back in the shop again and it almost feels like I've never left. I ended up coming in early. After being forced awake before my alarm went off this morning, there wasn't any point just sitting around, plus it was awkward after mine and Liam's weird disagreement, whatever that was about. I honestly don't care if he thinks I'm arrogant or ignorant or both because I don't like to watch the *bad* news. As I water the rubber plants then wipe the dust off their leaves, a pang of guilt hits me in the stomach as I remember Liam's peace offering of a bacon sandwich and cup of tea. That was sweet and it was also a very good sandwich. He is sort of trying to keep the peace, I suppose.

With an hour to go before we open, I potter about with the plants, watering them, rearranging them and repotting some of them before taking a few photos and videos for social media. With fifteen minutes to spare I flick the switch on the kettle, tilting my neck from side to side until I hear it click as I wait for the kettle to boil. A strong coffee is needed and I make just that before sitting down at the counter to gaze out onto the high street.

My eyes wander to the window and I sit up straight,

alert to the fact that The Shmoo and Mohawk Man, aka Mr Woodling, are walking past together. They know each other and I'm surprised to see them involved in a discussion. It looks friendly enough though. The Shmoo chucks his head back and laughs as Mr Woodling speaks intently whilst gesticulating with his hands. I'd love to know what they're talking about. In unison they both glance in the shop window, Mr Woodling gives a little wave and The Shmoo nods at his own reflection. They leave my line of vision and my thoughts turn to Willow and how she's been willing The Shmoo to come in to the shop for such a long time. I smile. The Shmoo got his nickname when Willow was staring out of the window one day. He bounced past all hair, limbs and boat shoes and I watched my friend as her mouth dropped open. Willow had meant to say, who is he? But the word who got stuck on her tongue and ended up sounding like *shmoo* and it's stuck ever since. It suits him. I miss my work pal, she may be my boss but she's also a great friend and brilliant company. We have a good laugh and although she's only been away a few days, I'm really beginning to feel her absence and her *what the fucculents*. I should ask her if she needs me to do anything in particular today, because there's only so much watering I can do. I bend down to pull my phone out of my bag.

'Are you open yet?' A shrill voice cuts across my thoughts and I look up to see an immaculate Missy Temple in her signature tweed jacket and skin tight jodhpurs with a cardboard box clasped in her perfectly manicured hands.

'Yes, just about.' I smile, hugging my coffee as Missy rearranges her face into a half smile, half grimace. Her makeup is perfect; flawless skin, smooth, full neutral lips and lashes that look long and natural but which are way too perfect to be real. I admire her face and beautiful hair, wondering how long it takes her to get ready in the morning when all I do is sling on my clothes, cover up any blemishes and spritz my curls back to life. She studies me with an almost twisty looking expression.

'Right, well I need to set up my pop-up shop.' She taps her foot and I nod obediently then jump down from my stool and walk over to the other side of the plant shop. She follows me and watches as I pull the cardboard box out from underneath the desk. She sets down the smaller cardboard box that she already has in her hands and delves into the one I give her, pulling out scarves, hats, gloves, leather belts and other little trinkets. She smiles at me, as if I've passed some sort of test.

'Okay, I'm going to set it all up, would you give me a hand with the signage? Please?' she says, thrusting a smaller box towards me.

As she's asked so nicely, I smile and say, 'Sure.' I follow her over to our agreed area and Missy lays everything out instructing me where to put the prices and signage. It surely must be taking her longer having to instruct me than to do it herself but I do as I'm told so as not to cause any annoyance to her. The last thing I want to do is upset a supplier, especially one that is here to entice in The Shmoo. Let's face it, we've already gotten off on the wrong foot, I don't want to rock the boat even further.

'Happy?' I ask, as we both stand back to appraise the display. It does look impressive. The scarves have been arranged in a rainbow fashion with trinkets at the end of the rainbow as if to imply they're the treasures in the ever-elusive bucket of gold. The beautifully knitted hats, gloves and leather belts sit on the smaller table. Everything is labelled up with the prices; everything is ready. Missy lets out a big huff and places her hands on her hips as she stares at the display.

'It will have to do, I hope you get the footfall to sell plenty,' she says eyeing me.

'Hopefully your lovely things will entice the customers in and we'll sell a few plants too,' I joke, in an attempt to lighten the mood. Missy stares at me, stony-faced.

'Yes, let's hope so,' she says, turning to look at her display.

We both stand awkwardly for a few moments before we're saved by the familiar ring of the shop door bell. It's Malcolm and he's arrived with freshly baked warm treats and probably some hot gossip. I wonder if he knows where Ravi has gone, I still haven't had a reply. He grins a toothy grin as he enters the shop, says hello then shifts on his feet expectantly.

'Hi Malc! How are you?' I smile, thankful for someone else in the shop.

'Yes, yes, good, good, can't complain.' He nods eagerly as his eyes shift between Missy and I.

'Oh sorry, where are my manners? Malc this is Missy, Missy this is Malcolm, he owns the bakery a few doors down.'

'Lovely to meet you, I've heard all about your talents,' he says, extending a hand forward to Missy.

'Likewise,' Missy says, as she feebly shakes his hand, unable to hide her disinterest as she avoids eye contact.

'Right well, my work here is done anyway, good luck with the sales.' Missy turns on her heel and clip clops out of the shop. The door dings and Malcolm and I both let out a sigh of relief.

'So glamorous,' Malc stage whispers, even though Missy is well out of ear shot.

'Hmmm,' I agree.

'What's she like? I've heard she's ever so sweet,' Malcolm says and I could laugh at the obvious digging for gossip. I want to say she's a complete snooty cow bag, but I don't.

'Yeah, she's nice, very sweet,' I say.

Malcolm is lovely and I love hearing the gossip and even more so his generous tasty treats but I don't want to give him any ammunition for gossip. As lovely as he is, I wouldn't trust him as far as I could throw him. If he's in here gossiping about everyone, no doubt he'll be down the road in someone else's shop gossiping about us. He thrusts a warm paper bag into my hands and I open it, closing my eyes to enjoy the sweet smell.

'Cinnamon and caramel swirls with a twist,' he says.

'What's the twist?' I smile.

'Ah,' Malcolm taps his nose. 'Secret family recipe.'

'Got you,' I say, as I take a bite, really not bothered whether I know about the twist or not. I'm hungry and his treats are always amazing.

'Hmmm, so good,' I say, in between mouthfuls, as Malcolm's eyes light up. 'Thank you so much.'

'Always a pleasure, You girls work hard, you deserve a treat. Where's Willow?'

'She's gone back home to see family, she'll be back next week.' I'll leave it to Willow to tell him, it feels wrong talking about her personal business with Malcolm even though I'm sure she wouldn't mind.

'Ahh, she didn't say she was going away,'

'Didn't she?'

'No. I have some bad news,' he says in a stage whisper, as his mouth turns upside down and his eyes widen.

'Bad news?' I say, as my voice goes up an octave. I

thought we were done with that for today.

'Yes, I'm afraid so, it could be very bad for business.' He looks around the shop for eavesdropping customers. The doorbell jingles and a lady walks in, both Malcolm and I smile and say hello as she begins to peruse the plants, walking straight past Missy's pop-up shop. Ha!

'What is it?' I whisper, getting slightly frustrated that Malcolm is almost making me beg for this bad news now. Just spit it out, I think, before stuffing another mouthful of Malcolm's swirl into my mouth. This stuff is too good, I swear it's how he manages to eek gossip out of people. Tricking them with treats.

'There's news of a new plant shop opening up in the spare premises down the road,' he whispers. 'It's early days and very hush hush. I'm not sure why it's so secret but rumours are circulating that Mr Woodling is the owner.'

'Really?' Oh shit. This is not good. Coolsbay is tiny and another plant shop could ruin us. My thoughts turn to him and the philodendron plant and I wonder if he'll be selling wonky plants in his shop.

'Yes, I wanted to tell Willow face to face, because you girls work so hard and Coolsbay is so small, there's really only room for one plant shop and that's Aloe Lovely.' He smiles over at the customer who smiles back. 'Greatest plant shop in Coolsbay,' he calls over to her, to my embarrassment.

'When is it supposed to open? Do you know anything else about it?' I whisper, hoping that Malcolm's being over dramatic and it's more likely a flower shop or just a shop that sells other things as well as a few plants. But a plant shop just like ours, that will matter, that could really damage us as a business.

'My source says within six weeks.' Just as Malcolm

says this the Shmoo walks past but this time without Mr Woodling in tow. He stops at the window by Missy's pop up, steps forward, smiles at his reflection, smooths down his hair and carries on his way. The suspicious over-thinking part of my brain wonders if The Shmoo has been spying on our shop for the purposes of market research and reporting back to Mr Woodling. I decide I most definitely need to get to know Mr Woodling now but for completely different reasons to my original ones. I have to ignore that he's easy on the eye and put on my business head. He can't fucculent with our shop.

I need to protect our Aloe Lovely.

Chapter 11

For the rest of the week thoughts of the shop being jeopardised hijack my thoughts.

As expected, and much to Missy Temple's dismay when she comes in at the end of the week to check, the footfall in the shop has been very slow but I did manage to sell the huge Monstera with thanks to a video I posted on social media that went semi-viral. I spent much of the week making more videos and even plucked up the courage to post a few live talking videos, guiding everyone around the shop. Every day, after I'd tidied, looked after the plants, ordered some new stock and/or updated the website, I set aside some time for social media and I have to say, it's really starting to pay off for the business. I even had Malcolm and a few others come in asking for advice. I did try to give Malcolm a hand with his marketing but he barely even uses a smart phone so it was rather challenging to say the least. He called himself an old dinosaur and I felt sorry for him so I offered to set him up on social media and get him started with a few videos and posts. After work one day we spent an hour videoing his tasty treats and the next day he had an order for a corporate gig in the next town that wanted a pastry breakfast, needless to say he was over the moon and so was I. Have I got a talent for this social media lark or is it just a fluke? The time I spent off work after Brandon left, glued to my phone, may have had a purpose.

The detailed handover to Willow that I've just written stares back at me as a sudden rush of satisfaction comes over me. Now, I can relax in the knowledge that I've done a good job with the shop this week. I can now look forward to my uni reunion. Except I'm really not, I'm actually panicking. Big time. I've booked a fucking male escort. What in the actual hell is wrong with me? My pulse quickens. In just a few hours I'm potentially going to see my ex-boyfriend that I haven't heard from or seen in six months apart from the lame monthly generic blogs and emails. I don't think my guts can handle this.

My mouth becomes dry as my stomach continually flips over and over as I try to concentrate on getting ready and making myself look as gorgeous as possible for the reunion. I've opted for a long black tight dress, killer heels and hair down and wild. Ex always said he liked my hair down, even though he admitted he preferred it straight, but it's raining so straightening it will be completely pointless. Curly hair will have to do, it's me anyway and if he doesn't like it, he can lump it.

Do I really want him back after he buggered off to *find* himself? My mind flashes back to our cosy home and weekends dining on Coolsbay harbour, drinking more than both of us could handle. Was our relationship just a drunken blur, we both never really stopped the uni style drinking that brought us together in freshers week. I pull my phone out of my handbag and open up the folder marked *do not open* in my emails. France, Spain, Turkey, India, Thailand and now Australia. I re-read each email, just in case I missed him asking how I was but no, nothing, no personal message or email just to me. Just generic boastful blogs.

The finishing touch to my outfit is a beautiful silver hairclip that Brandon bought me years ago. I slide it into one side of my hair after finally deciding that it won't be weird if I wear it, it's just a hair clip and he won't remember that he bought it for me, men don't remember these things, do they? I slather on another coating of lip gloss then arrange myself on the sofa to wait for my escort. To begin with, I try to concentrate on the latest episode of *Stranger Things* but with a whole hour to go until Eddie the escort arrives, my mind is racing. I check my bag, unpack and pack again then end up pacing up and down the living room with the TV on full blast, streaming Kate Bush music videos off *YouTube*. I begin to walk my best walk, singing at the top of my lungs to try and calm myself down. It's cathartic and I'm really enjoying myself singing along to *The Hounds of Love*, I'd heard a couple of her songs before as Dad used to listen to her a bit when we were growing up but since her music has featured on *Stranger Things*, I've bought all her albums. *Wuthering Heights* is on next and I pace up and down aiming for the high notes and stretching my arms out wide just like Kate does. I'm just singing about being let into the window, miming being stuck outside when a familiar voice booms.

'Don't give up your day job, please.'

The nerves and excitement cause me to stop dead in my tracks and scream right into Liam's shocked face. 'Arrrghhhh.' What the hell is he doing home?

'Jesus Christ woman, was that part of the performance? It's a bit pitchy at best.' He laughs, doubling over at his own joke and I want to punch him. The last thing I want is for him to be hanging about when

Eddie gets here. This was not in the plan. I booked Eddie for this time safe in the knowledge that everyone would be at work and I could meet him without any questions. Now Liam is here, I'm going to have to think of a way to get rid of him.

'Oh, shut up. You scared me. You can't just creep up on people like that,' I say, as the smirk slowly disappears from his face.

He's filthy as usual, covered in paint and dust. He uses his white t-shirt to wipe his forehead and I turn away as he flashes his perfectly toned abs. He may have a lovely stomach but he's a cocky arse.

'Umm, I live here and it was hardly creeping, didn't you hear the door go?' he asks, and I shake my head, still panting from the shock of him being here. 'Where are you going dressed like that anyway?' He slowly looks me up and down and I try to steady my breathing.

'Dressed like what? You sound like my dad.' I laugh as he meets my eyes with a hint of a smile playing across his lips.

'No, I mean you look nice but umm…' he falters and if I didn't know him better, I'd say he was a tad flustered by me. Liam stuck for words is definitely a first.

'But what?' I say, tilting my head and smiling, enjoying making him uncomfortable.

He grins and raises both eyebrows, looking at me with those twinkling yet goading blue eyes. 'You're all done up in the day time, what is it? A granny's disco? A spot of bingo?' His usual cocky demeanour resumes and I shift on my feet, the heels already feeling a bit uncomfortable. The fact that he thinks I'm a bit of a granny annoys me.

'No. I have my ten-year uni reunion,' I say, checking my watch. 'It's in Manchester so that's why I'm ready.

I'm leaving in a bit and it's a long drive so. . .' Go away.

'Ahh right, sounds fun.'

'Yep, it will be.' More than you know, I think. I check my watch again. Just half an hour until he gets here. How can I get Liam out of the house?

'Just gonna make some lunch, you want anything?' he asks.

'Oh, are you going back to work then?' I ask, sounding probably too hopeful.

'No, I'm done for the day, it's Friday.' He frowns then proceeds to offer a little dance of joy, gyrating his hips and waving his hands above his head. He's got moves I'll give him that.

'Right. Umm, no thank you, I'm good.'

'Suit yourself,' he says as he stops dancing. 'I'll just make one delicious brioche burger with tomatoes, cheese and pickled gherkins then.' He studies my face and I gulp down saliva.

Why do I always forget to eat? This is why I overeat. I forget to eat and get so ravenous that I have enormous meals to make up for it. A cave woman, I eat like a pre-historic cave woman who never knows where she will get her next meal from. Another thing I need to work on. It's endless. I wonder how NextlevelNyssa eats, probably all vegan based and perfectly healthy regular, balanced meals.

Oh, bore off, Nyssa.

'Yeah, you know, I'm feeling rather faint, quite ill even,' I croak, as I sit down and put my head between my legs desperately trying to snatch some time to hatch a quick 'get rid of Liam' plan.

'Stay there. I'll get you a glass of water,' he says and leaves the room. Moments later he's back with a pint glass of water.

'Here you go.'

I lift my head up and he puts the glass to my lips, feeding me like a wounded baby bird.

'Thanks.' I feebly take a sip then put my hand to my head. 'Ouch. Oh no I feel a migraine coming on, I need my tablets but I've run out, will you go to the shop for me?' I gaze into his eyes and blink slowly as I bite my bottom lip. 'Please?'

'Right, okay,' he says, as I check my watch again. Fifteen minutes, if I can get him out of the house now then that gives me enough time to get him to the shop. I'll have to immediately leave with Eddie but that will be fine, no need to hang about. 'I'll check the cupboards first, shall I? Surely there's something in there we can use,' he continues.

'Ummm no, I need the pink bombs.'

'The pink bombs? Sounds ominous.'

'Yeah, they're like super strength pain killers, the only thing that stops it from turning into a full-on migraine,' I say, with my hand on my head. I'm certain I don't have any pink bombs so he will definitely have to go to the shop then I can make my quick escape. I take a quick glance at my watch again; ten minutes to go. My heart races in my chest, why am I behaving so unhinged about this? As far as Liam is concerned this guy is just a normal date coming to my uni reunion, it's not weird or strange, I have nothing to feel anxious about. And yet I do feel weird and eaten up with anxiety because *I know* that I've hired an escort and I'm worried that Liam will somehow see through that. He's got those penetrating accusing eyes. I need to get him out of the house so I don't have to think about *him*.

'Please, I need the pink bombs,' I whine from the living room, as I listen to cupboards and drawers opening in the kitchen. There's a few moments of silence interspersed with the sound of bottles chinking together and the rustling of packets. Then Liam appears with a packet of pills in hand.

'Bingo!' he says, waving the packet of pink bombs at me.

Shit. Shit. Shit.

'Wow, where did you find them?' I croak.

'Kathy the walking pharmacy of course.' He winks. 'Your drawer was pathetic, only things in there were cough medicine from like five years ago and a packet of women's multi vitamins for good skin, teeth and hair. Ah, I found this odd contraption too, he holds up my blackhead buster that I bought off *Facebook* last year after watching the amazing results videos. It actually isn't great and apart from scraping many layers of my skin off, it didn't get rid of the small cluster of blackheads on my nose that no one else can see but have always bugged me. Shit. I knew I should have kept that safe in my room. 'What is it?' he asks, turning it around in his hand as I pray to the gods that I washed it after I used it.

'I don't know, it's not mine,' I lie. Five minutes to go. I'm doomed. Just as I think this the doorbell rings. There's nothing for it, I'll just have to face the music.

'I'll get it, probably that overkeen Jehovah Witness again,' Liam says, as I leap up from my seat, all signs of a migraine forgotten. He throws me a weird look then heads towards the door.

I stand for a moment and then begin to collect my things together, handbag, travel bag, phone, purse, keys. Done. Time to escape out of the door with one escort in tow.

'Urrrm, it's for you.' Liam's eyebrows knit together before a small smile plays across his lips. Why is he bloody smiling?

'Thanks,' I say, as I rush towards the door with my bags. I leave the pills on the table then quickly snatch them back as I notice Liam eyeing me suspiciously. This really isn't going well. Never mind, soon I'll be up in Manchester having the time of my life catching up with old friends, with a hot man in tow, making Brandon jealous.

'Hey,' I say, pasting on a winning smile as I come face to face with the escort. 'Eddie?' I ask because he doesn't look like the guy in the profile or maybe he is but just two decades older. He's wearing an oversized suit, slicked back hair and has a pin on his lapel of a pink flamingo.

Oh fucculent.

'Ello treacle, nice to meet you, care for a mint?' Eddie the escort says in a broad East End accent as he leans forward offering an ancient looking packet of polos that look like they've been retrieved from the nineteen-eighties. I try to stop my jaw from dropping to the floor. Liam who is hovering behind me, sniggers into my neck. I'm taking Del Boy from *Only Fools and Horses* to my uni reunion.

'No, no thank you. I'm fine thanks, but I've just got to pop to the loo first.'

Oh God, this couldn't get any worst. I'm calling the bloody escort agency, there's no way I can take Del Boy from *Only Fools and Horses* to my uni reunion, I'll get laughed out of the building. People will think that he's my dad at best and my husband at worst. I can't do this; I don't want to do this. I should never have booked him. What the hell was I thinking? I cuss myself for being such a sap for tarot card readings. Never again. I should just learn to listen to my intuition, just like NextlevelNyssa advised.

Sorry Nyssa, you were right.

Closing the bathroom door behind me, I sit down on the toilet lid and begin to tap on my phone. The escort agencies website pops up and I frantically tap backwards and forwards trying to find a contact number. It's impossible to find a phone number, there's nothing on the webpage, just an email address and by the time someone replies it will be too late. Nevertheless, I type a quick email.

To whoever this may concern,

Eddie007 needs his profile updating. Not as advertised. As least ten years behind on the photos. Would not recommend. I would like a refund as I will be unable to continue my date with him due to the false advertising. Please respond to me asap. Charlotte Price.

I tap send then instantly feel bad. It's not Eddie's fault. Who am I kidding? Of course it is, he must have allowed them to use those pics. I scroll the internet once more desperately trying to find a number for the escort agency but no such luck. I need to go back out there and let Eddie down gently. Getting up, I splash a bit of cold water on my wrists, I'd splash my face too but I have a lot of makeup on. I stare back at the idiot in the mirror who thought this would be a good idea.

'You really are a moron do you know that,' I say to my reflection, as she stares back at me looking bemused. I take a few deep breaths then open the bathroom door and pad back towards the front door. I stop in my tracks after hearing muffled voices as I reach the living room door, standing still with my ear to the door I listen to Liam and Eddie. He must have invited him in. They're talking about football. Of course.

'Alright treacle, feeling better now?' Eddie growls, putting his hands behind his head and smoothing down his already slick hair as I walk into the room.

Liam looks between us both and I feel my hand fling up to my head again.

'Actually no, I'm feeling very unwell,' I wail.

'Oh no, sorry to hear that, babe,' Eddie says with concern, and a twang of guilt hits me again about my complaint. 'Yeah, I think I'm going to have to cancel.'

'Are you sure? I'm great at playing doctors and nurses.' He leers before a hacking cough ensues. Okay, now I don't feel so bad.

'She is unwell mate, stank the whole house out before you got here.'

'Ahh that's rank,' says Del Boy as his face twists in disgust.

'Yeah, and she has some pretty gross habits too.'

'Like what?'

'The worst kind.' Liam acts out picking his nose and eating it. Never have I ever wanted to punch him more yet also hug him at the same time. It's a strange feeling.

Eddie looks to me and I shrug as if to say, sorry, it can't be helped. 'I'm just a dirty shit stinking snot gobbler.' I confess as Liam looks away trying to hide his sniggering. 'I'm a dirty nose picker and eater. The worst kind of woman.'

'Okay, well I'm out of here then, get better soon,' he says, without looking at me. 'Thanks for the hospitality, geezer.' Eddie fist pumps Liam and races towards the front door and I grimace as Liam's eyes move to mine. He shakes his head slowly.

I have a lot to answer for.

Chapter 12

'Who in the hell was that *geezer* and why was I saving you from him?' Liam mocks in his best East End London accent which leaves much to be desired, as he eyes me questioningly from the sofa. A hint of a smirk plays across his lips and I watch him fold his arms behind his neck.

I have to avert my eyes as his t-shirt rides up to reveal his toned, tanned stomach complete with a smattering of light brown hair. This was not how it was meant to go. I should be en-route to Manchester with a hot guy in tow, not this.

'Oh God,' I say, slapping my forehead with both hands which then slide down to cover most of my face. I want to hide away. My once perfect makeup melting. 'This is a disaster,' I mumble into my fingers, then peer through them to find Liam leaning forward, tilting his head, looking curiously at me. I suppose I owe him some sort of explanation.

'I can see that it's become a bit ummm… hectic,' he says finally, carefully choosing a word to describe this odd situation in which he's had to fend off a strange man who doesn't appear to know me.

'That's one word for it,' I say. 'It's my uni reunion

today and Eddie was coming with me as my chaperone, if you like. I didn't want to go alone. Brandon is going to be there and I wanted a bit of support, a bit of company to travel down with and for when I met with the others.' I don't say it's because I have nothing to show for the past ten years and Eddie was going to be my crutch to lean on.

'Right, and how do you know this Eddie?'

'Does it matter how I know him? We were put in contact through mutual friends and he obviously wasn't suitable for the reunion,' I snap, feeling stressed and embarrassed at the whole situation.

'Ah, kind of like a blind date?' Liam asks.

'Yeah,' I lie. Well, I can't tell him that I hired an escort can I? How incredibly sad and desperate does that sound? I mean I know I am a bit but *he* doesn't have to know.

'Where's your reunion?' he asks.

'Manchester,' I say gloomily. 'But I'm not going to go now, that's just put a whole dampener on it. I'm really *not* in the mood.' My heart sinks as I think of the uni girls' faces when I tell them I can't make it; it's been years since we all caught up properly and I was so looking forward to it, especially catching up with Lydia and Kate, my besties. Eddie was just meant to slot into the background and act as a sort of hot body guard.

'Right, well, I could come with you,' Liam says slowly, in his soft Irish lilt. 'I'm not doing anything else this weekend.'

'Thanks, but no, I'm not going to go.'

'Oh, come on, you're going to let big dickhead energy win are you? Let's go and show that tool what he's been missing,' he says, with a lazy lop-sided grin. 'You look great, Grotty. Great outfit.' He eyes me up and down and a shiver rises up my neck.

'It's big dick energy and no thank you, I'm so over it now.'

'Fine, suit yourself but wouldn't you just love to see the look on his face when he sees us two together?' Liam says, as a glint appears in his eyes. I bring my knees up to my chest and rest my chin on them. 'He's never been a fan of me, has he?' he continues. 'And it would be so amusing to watch his face trying to fill in the gaps.'

'Hmmm, maybe.' He's right, Brandon has never been a fan, a few years ago they ended up playing football together and Brandon would always bitch about him afterwards, which in turn made me dislike Liam more.

'It would, come on, don't be defeated by him. Let's make him feel a little bit of what you must have been feeling these last few months.'

My mind wanders to the day he sort of broke up with me and the sad turn of events that have spiralled along from it ever since. Perhaps it is time to take back what is mine and by that I don't necessarily mean him. I mean my self-respect and dignity, because God knows how many crying voicemails and long texts I left him, only to receive a generic email meant for everyone, not his long-term girlfriend who he'd just abandoned without a care in the world. I think of all the money I've spent on tarot card readings just to have that glimmer of hope and to be told that he'd come back to me some day. Suddenly I feel something that I haven't felt before in all these months. I feel angry. Why should he get to enjoy all the fun, he's already taken enough away from me. My life has been on hold for the last six months.

'Fine, but there will be a few conditions.' I stand up with a new fire ignited in my belly. Bringing myself up to my full five-foot-two inches and flicking my mane of hair behind my shoulders, I glare at Liam, is he up to it?

'Hit me.' Liam leans his arms on his knees and knits his fingers together.

'No calling me Grotty for starters or any other lame nickname, it's Lottie or Charlotte and that's it.'

'Got it.' He nods.

'No embarrassing stories from when we were younger. You have to be on my team, we come as one, a union, so that means you big me up whenever possible, especially when *he* is in earshot.'

'Goes without saying.' Liam nods.

'People may think we're together and that's okay for them to assume that.' I make a wincing face that Liam mirrors back at me. He opens his mouth to talk and I hold my hand up to stop him. 'Just because they assume that we're together,' I say, using inverted comma air signs on the word 'together'. 'It doesn't give you free reign to touch me, you may put a simple arm around me from time to time but absolutely no need for hand holding, that's too much, and kissing is most definitely out of the question.'

Liam sticks his fingers down his throat and pretends to gag. My pride prickles a little. He must really think I am Grotty but I don't care, he will serve a purpose whilst we're there although I'm not too sure why he's so keen to come along other than to wind up Brandon, who we now share a sort of mutual hatred for. I narrow my eyes at him, suddenly suspicious of his motives.

'Why are you so keen to come along anyway?' I ask, staring down at him as I move my hands onto my hips. An image of Liam on our kitchen floor when we were kids flashes into my mind's eye. I think Harry punched him once for teasing me and making me cry and we had to call an ambulance. He was fine though, no real damage done, apart from pride, we didn't see him much after that.

'Why not? I bloody love a good road trip. I get itchy feet staying in one place for too long, Coolsbay can be so dull at times and for once I haven't any plans this weekend.' He leans back again and folds his arms behind his head whilst I concentrate hard on not looking at his teasing midriff.

'Okaaay.'

'Also, I love Manchester and you never know when I might need to save you or one of your hot friends from choking on a peanut.' He winks and a flashback of his strong arms around my waist sear into my thoughts. 'I'll be your uni reunion Irish superhero.' He flexes his biceps then roars with laughter at himself. He really is a bit of an idiot.

'Okay, don't get too carried away. I'd be perfectly fine without you,' I say, considering if this is a good move. Can I really put up with this arrogance for a whole twenty-four hours?

'Remember, you weren't going to go alone and let's face it, it would be a whole lot better with me.' His eyebrows dance about on his face then he grins a wicked grin that makes him look like a bit like an evil villain. He looks so ridiculous that I can't help but let out a burst of laughter. It will be fun to see the look on Brandon's face, that's for sure.

'Fine.' I toss him a set of keys. 'But you're driving the hire car.'

By the time we've faffed around getting Liam put on the car insurance coupled with me sorting my face out again, we're almost two hours behind schedule. I've text Kate and Lydia to tell them I'm running late but I'm on my way. I consider telling them that I'm bringing a male companion, but don't. It will be a nice surprise for everyone. They both send back squealing voice notes, hysteria setting in already that the gang will finally be back together, plus my chaperone Liam.

'So, what did you do at uni again?' Liam asks, cutting across my thoughts as we exit the motorway. I smile a nostalgic smile.

'Music production.'

'What?'

'Yeah, I know, I hadn't a clue what I wanted to do and it looked fun in the prospectus so I chose that.'

'Fair enough,' he says. 'I still don't know what I want to do and I'm approaching middle-aged hood.'

'Thirty-four isn't middle-aged these days, you're middle-aged around fifty now,' I say. 'It was actually really, really hard; my degree I mean. Even though I was a bit crap at it, the uni part was fun, I was definitely good at the socialising bit and the meeting my partner bit.' I wince at my own bitter sweet comment, what a good partner he turned out to be. 'I scraped a 2:2 so on paper it didn't look too bad to potential employers. Even if a music degree has nothing to do with being someone's PA, it meant something then.'

'Didn't fancy becoming the next Simon Cowell then?' He snorts.

'Nah, but Pete Waterman came and did a talk at our university, he said that less than five percent of people who do a media degree will actually end up working in media. A lot of people cried into their cheeky *Vimtos* at the student union bar that night.'

'Who's Pete Waterman?'

'Are you from this planet? He's a music producer amongst many other things. He judged *the* first UK reality singing contest.'

Liam glances at me blankly before turning his attention back to the road.

'*Pop Idol.*' I was only a kid but Mum and Dad used to let me stay up late to watch it. The best thing on TV at the time.

'Nope.' Liam shakes his head.

'He helped put together *Girls Aloud* for Christ's sake.' I laugh then hold up a finger, remembering. 'Ah, Louis Walsh was also a judge and he actually first managed *Girls Aloud.*'

'Just because you name a fellow Irishman it doesn't mean the memory of an awful reality show with probably equally awful singing will come back to me. I never watched any of those reality shows.'

'What did you watch then?' I'm pretty sure that's all that existed in the early naughties on UK TV screens. Reality TV and *The X Files.*

'What year was it?'

'I think it was 2001-2003.'

'Probably Eurotrash or something.' He laughs. 'I don't know, it was a really long time ago.'

'Yes, it was.' A core memory of Liam and my brother's mates skating over to me at the local ice rink slides into my thoughts. Moments later I was in the toilets crying because Liam had sprayed ice all over me causing me to fall over and face plant the rink floor. That was humiliating and I didn't see him for a while after that because Harry was cross with him. A few months later all was forgiven and he was back in our house, behaving like a moron. I turn up the radio, not in the mood to chat anymore. Ironically *Girls Aloud's* Cheryl begins to blare out of the speakers singing something about calling her name. We sit in silence for a few minutes, Liam mumbles something about turning off absolute rubbish and listening to some real music. He twiddles with the radio before settling on a rock station playing *Guns and Roses*. I reach into my handbag to message Willow.

Me: *Hey, how's it going in the shop? Hope you're okay. Xx.* I keep my phone in my hand for a good ten minutes, watching out of the window at the bleak winter views until it buzzes with her reply.

Willow: *I'm not too bad thanks, Chick. The shop is busy! Don't know what you did but I bloody love you for it. Thank you. The Shmoo is so close to entering the building, I can just feel it. He's walked past and smiled at me a few times. Missy's stock is lovely and we've sold a few scarves and a couple of pairs of gloves but not as much as I thought. The plants are doing well though.*

That'll be my social media posts then. The Instagram one did particularly well; when I last checked it had more than twenty clicks to the website.

Me: *That's amazing! I'm so pleased. Come on The Shmoo! I'm en-route to Manchester. Update on the escort. Del Boy from Only Fools and Horses turned up minus the charm and the gold jewellery so I sent him packing, taking Liam instead.*

Willow: *The flat mate that stole your bedroom and tormented you as a child?*

Me: *Yeah, him. I'll fill you in when I'm back. xx*

I slide my phone into my bag and check the time. We've been on the road an hour, just three more to go until we get there.

'Want to play a game?' Liam asks, sensing my boredom. After finally leaving the country roads, we're now on another motorway so the drive is bleak and with the winter rain, it's much less than scenic.

'Sure, what is it?'

'You've got to try and get someone's phone number by the time we get to the first service station in about an hour. Then, we'll swap over, you'll drive and it can be my turn. Whoever gets the most phone numbers wins.'

'Right, what do they win?' I laugh.

'They win,' he pauses, thinking about his answer.

'I win my bedroom back?' I cut in with a grin.

'No way, you aren't even paying Harry rent, try again.'

'Comes with being a sister territory. Okay, maybe that's slightly unfair.'

'What about if I win, you have to be my house slave for a week, that means, cooking me all my meals, doing my washing and whatever else I ask within the realms of looking after me.' He grins a big cheeky grin before changing gear and I shake my head.

'Okay, but a week is a bit steep. Let's settle for seventy-two hours and of course, it's vice versa, if I win you have to be my slave.' An image of being force fed pickled gherkins whilst arranging and sorting all my makeup pops into my mind and I snort to myself. It will take him hours. Days even.

'Seventy-two hours and you have yourself a deal,' he says as he offers me a chewing gum.

'Fine.' I stuff the chewing gum into my mouth.

Let the competition begin.

Chapter 13

'Wait, I've agreed to this but how am I supposed to get phone numbers from inside a car on the motorway?'

Why did I agree to this? It's a stupid game. A game for immature teenagers really but it will pass the time during the long drive up to Manchester and keep my mind off the reunion and potentially seeing Brandon which is imminent and already giving me extreme hives. I take a big bite of my pickled gherkin, taking comfort in the familiar tasty tanginess on my tongue. I'm going to see him again and I need to forget about that for now because it's doing me no good.

'You've got to use your imagination,' he says slowly in a croaky voice, before cranking up the radio and the heating. He sniffs the air and makes a disgusted-slash-amused face at me.

'Okay,' I say obligingly, as I rummage in my handbag for my makeup and Liam offers me another chewing gum. I apply a few more layers of bright pink lipstick, check my eyebrows for any strays and my teeth for any bits. I spray a bit of curl reviver into my hands and zhoosh up my hair a bit. All good. Now what?

The next thirty minutes consists of me gazing out of the window watching the cars whizz by as I search for potential number givers. It's going to be hard to get a man to trust me because I have one sitting next to me and I think they'll wonder what I'm up to but it will be even harder for Liam. Women tend to stick together more and he's basically cock blocking me. Apart from the fact this whole game is giving me whiplash I'm feeling pretty confident that as soon as we slow down, I'll be able to woo someone with a seductive look. Let's hope so anyway. Finally we hit roadworks. We slow down to fifty miles per hour and then down to thirty miles per hour in lanes of three and a car load of five lads in their mid-late twenties pull up next to us. I lean forward slightly to block out Liam and turn to face them, one of them whips his head around to look in and the others shortly follow suit. I give them my best and what I think is a charming smile. A couple of the men smile back and then there's a bit of (what I think is) excited banter amongst the group. I can't hear what they're saying but I imagine it to be something along the lines of *she's alright boys, think we've pulled.* Now how do I get a phone number from this if they can't hear me? We exchange a few more smiles and glances, with the youngest looking lad, in a red jumper catching my eye more than the others. I decide to focus on him.

'Phone number,' I mouth at him with a nod and a smile, and he frowns then shakes his head, he's still smiling though. Clearly, he doesn't know what I've just said. 'Phone number,' I try again when he glances back, this time waving my phone at him.

'They can't hear you, desperate woman.' Liam sniggers.

'Shut up, don't interrupt my game,' I snap.

'And they certainly wouldn't be giving you their phone number if they could smell your gherkin breath,' he says, as I wind down the window and he offers me another chewing gum. I ignore him and wiggle my phone at the red jumper lad again but this time he turns away.

Snubbed.

The others I notice are all laughing, I wiggle my phone at them and say 'Phone number.' Well, I may as well try whilst they're there. They carry on laughing, pushing each other. Hysterical.

'Oh fuck. This is humiliating,' I say, sliding back down into my chair as low as I can go until I'm almost sitting in the footwell. Facing forward, I stay there until they finally go away whilst Liam pisses himself with laughter along with them. 'You're an absolute arse of the highest order and you aren't going to win this,' I spit from the comfort of the hire cars footwell. There is no way I am being this man's slave for seventy-two hours. The competition is on but maybe I'll tone down the desperation a bit. Less is more. 'I think you put them off,' I accuse, when we speed up again. 'Just you being there, makes them question why a girl travelling with her boyfriend would be asking for a random man's phone number.'

'No, they could definitely smell that pickled breath.' He laughs. 'Harder than you thought, hey?' He grins then glances at me, his ice blue eyes twinkling with humour.

'Yes,' I reluctantly agree, whilst trying not to grit my teeth. Less is more. Less is more, Lottie. You've got this.

It's a while until we slow down again, in the meantime we discuss Liam's charity work and the fact that he literally wants to be a nomad and travel the world forever helping others in need. He said he's found his purpose in life and good for him. We argue about which radio channel to listen to, me wanting *Kiss* and him wanting *Rock FM* until we finally agree that we'll stream my

Spotify and listen to *Kate Bush* albums.

'I'm surprised you like her,' I say.

'Why? She's great. Women's work was my mother's favourite, we played it at her funeral.'

'Ah, I'm sorry, I didn't know she'd passed.'

'Yep, a very long time ago now, I was a teenager, went a bit off the rails after that, that's when I went back to Ireland for a few years,' he says all matter-of-fact, and a vague recollection of Harry telling me that Liam's mum had died comes back to me and I feel awful for forgetting. He must have gone through a lot.

'Sorry Liam, that must have been really rough for you.' Shit has just got deep.

'It's kind of ironic really.' A wry smile plays across his lips as he changes gear and loosens his grip on the steering wheel. 'The song says about having *a little life left in you yet* but she didn't have any life in her, not at all, because she was already dead.' His shoulders begin to shake and I rest my hand on his arm. Poor Liam. His eyes crinkle up in amusement then a high-pitched strangled hyena-like giggle escapes his mouth. It sounds so funny, so out of character, that a burst of laughter escapes me too.

'No. We can't laugh at your dead mum,' I say, through tears of laughter.

'Yes, we can. What a terrible song choice. She chose it too, probably to taunt us or something.' He smiles, nostalgically. 'She always said she'd come back and haunt us if she thought we were misbehaving. She was an amazing woman, the heart of the family.' He glances down at his leg and bites his lip. To my horror my hand has slid onto his thigh to comfort him. I pull it away quickly to scratch a non-existent itch on my nose.

'I bet she'd be proud of you,' I say quietly, as I turn to

look out of the window.

'You think?' He glances at me and smiles a funny smile.

'Yeah.' I smile back before returning my eyeline to the road out of the passenger window. We've slowed down again and there's an older man driving a van alongside us. It's time to lighten the mood and get a phone number.

Less than two minutes later and mission accomplished.

'I'm not sure if I can let you have that one?' Liam squints his eyes at me and I shake my head at him.

'You didn't stipulate previously in the rules so I'm afraid it does count,' I counter, as I give the driver a little wave and a thumbs up. 'Anyway, it is always handy to know a good plumber,' I add.

'We're almost two hours away from Coolsbay so he'd have to turn the water into gold to make it worth your while,' Liam remarks, as a snigger escapes me.

'Well, you never know.'

The next thirty minutes whizz by as I up my game and focus on getting as many phone numbers as I can. I get another three numbers including a Brummy boy racer who wants to take me for a ride in his car, a flash business man in a Merc who was over the moon when I asked him and a woman who was advertising her hair dressing services but only had her social media handles on her car. I told her I didn't do social media so would like her phone number instead. Needless to say, Liam wasn't pleased about that one and said I'd cheated again. So that's 4 – 0 to me. I feel slightly guilty that these people may be looking forward to receiving a call from me but it has been a laugh and something to pass the time. We pull up to the Midlands service station and go our separate ways to freshen up. By the time I've got back to the car Liam is surrounded by five girls who are lapping up whatever Irish charm twaddle is coming out of his mouth.

'Yeah, so she's back now ladies and shhhh remember don't be spoiling the surprise. I'll get in touch with you girls soon,' I hear him say with a wink as I approach his side and he slings an arm around me.

'Spoil what surprise?' I smile at him as I gently remove his arm from around my shoulder before making eye contact with the other girls. The fake relationship hasn't started yet, cheeky. A few of them giggle but no one says anything, instead they just eye me curiously and smile. Apart from one who has a face like a slapped arse. There's always one. She folds her arms and frowns at Liam before looking me up and down.

'Oh, nothing, *is* it ladies?' Liam says, arching an eyebrow.

'No nothing,' they all chorus, apart from slapped-arse face who keeps her jaw clenched shut; she reminds me of Missy Temple. We climb into the car and I stare at him in bemusement with my hands on the steering wheel.

'What were you talking about just now?' I ask.

'I can't reveal my secrets I'm afraid, my dear, Charlotte,' he says, smoothly tapping his nose. 'But I can reveal that I have just collected four phone numbers,' he adds smugly.

'What?' I shriek, incredulous. I want to punch him but there's something in the way that he said Charlotte that makes my spine tingle and my face heat up despite my annoyance, maybe this is what extreme annoyance feels like but it feels oddly nice.

'Sorry.' He shrugs, not sorry at all. I start the car, huffing and turn the car radio to something poppy that I know will hurt his ears. I know I'm being petty but I really don't want to be this man's slave. He's a clearly a sadist, he'll have me polishing his work boots at six in the morning with my tongue.

We drive in silence for the next hour, only an hour to go and then we'll be there. My heart starts to beat faster in my chest.

'You haven't tried to get another phone number,' I acknowledge, desperately trying to distract myself from my own anxiety.

'Nah, I'm in no rush,' he replies breezily. 'Just one more phone number and I'm the winner and you're the slave for a whole seventy-two hours.'

I grip the steering wheel, grit my teeth and stare ahead. Why did I agree to this? Ten minutes pass and we slow right down into a traffic jam, gridlocked. Liam rolls his window down and pokes his head out to see what's going on.

'Ahh shite, it's a little granny, looks like she's been in an accident maybe,' Liam says.

'Oh no. Is anyone helping her?' I ask.

'Dunno, can't see yet.' We creep further along the road until we come to what we thought was an accident. A little old lady has broken down and the AA are fixing her car. I don't know why this is causing gridlock as she is on the hard shoulder but maybe it's because the car had to be pushed over to the side of the road and God knows how long that might have taken.

'At least she's getting help,' Liam says, and I agree then sigh heavily, feeling sorry for the little old lady and frustrated at the long drive. My stomach growls. This is going to take much longer than expected. 'Can you grab my smaller bag from the back? I have some snacks.'

'Sure,' Liam reaches into the backseat and a fresh waft

of wood and cinnamon infiltrates my nostrils. He passes me the bag and I reach in for the brownies I made last night, pulling off the lid. These will certainly fill a gap. I stuff one into my mouth, offering one to Liam who takes two, well I guess they are small. We're now adjacent to the little old lady's car and I can see worry etched on her face as the AA men peer into her bonnet, scratching their heads and then their bums.

'Aww bless her, she looks freezing,' I say, with a shiver feeling upset for this poor woman. 'I've got a blanket in the boot, let's give it to her,' I add, as my pitch gets higher, I want to make her feel better in some way. We're stationary so I pop the boot of the hire car.

'Good plan, batman,' Liam says, as he jumps out of the car and pulls the blanket out of the boot. He begins to walk over there and I call after him.

'Here, take these, too.' I push the tub of brownies into his arms along with an unopened bottle of water and he looks at me with a strange expression. Sort of impressed but also confused, I think. He trots off and I watch him as the old lady appears to coo over his helpfulness. I don't mind that they think it's him that's been helpful, after all he does the real charity work all the time. I enjoy watching the exchange until he jogs back to the car with an empty plastic tub.

'She said to say thank you, she was starting to feel weak because she suffers from low blood pressure and that drink and brownies will really hit the spot, she's already drunk the water.' I look over to see her wrapped up in the blanket happily chatting with the AA men. I catch her eye and give her a little wave and she begins to frantically wave and talk at me.

'Roll down the window, she's trying to say something,' I say. Liam does as requested as the dear old lady shouts from the side of the road.

'Thank you so much dear for the blanket and these brownies are delightful,' she says, smacking her lips before licking her fingers, making sure to savour every crumb.

'No problem, hope you get home and your car gets sorted soon.' I smile.

'Me too. Honestly, they are just divine, I'd ask you for the recipe if you weren't about to drive off,' she titters.

'No worries,' I shout. 'Just give me your phone number and I'll text it to you, it's really no problem.' Liam and I watch as the lady faffs about for a pen and paper, ordering the AA men to sort it for her.

'Thanks love, great brownies.' One of the AA men comes running over with her phone number as impatient cars begin to beep behind us.

'You planned that, you sly woman.' Liam laughs as we slowly drive off.

'I did not. Just saw an opportunity,' I say, but actually I forgot all about the game and collecting phone numbers. I was having too much fun making someone smile.

Chapter 14

It's almost seven o'clock by the time we finally arrive at the hotel. It certainly looks a lot grander than it does on the inside but then again it is dark. The outside resembles a fancy, classy establishment with Georgian decor and twinkly lights. The inside resembles a throw back to the seventies, everything, including the lamp shades and bed spreads, are varying shades of brown next to orange pine furniture. It almost makes me feel nauseous.

The reunion, already in full swing, started even earlier than originally planned. Kate texted me to say that they were all there at six thirty in the hotel bar. She said some people met even earlier. We check into the room and I cringe at the fact we're sharing. At least it's two single beds with a table in between them and a spacious, albeit wooden, bathroom. How I ever thought it was going to be okay sharing with Del Boy is beyond me; I clearly wasn't thinking straight. It was a panic purchase, except that rather than it being the usual panic buy such as an item of clothing, a tarot reading, a plant or a piece of jewellery to make myself feel better, it was a person. I've now learnt my lesson. You should never buy, or rather panic choose, a person. It isn't that odd to be sharing with Liam, he is already my housemate and I know he's not a complete freak so that's a bonus too.

'So does the slave prize start now? My shoes could do with a polish.'

I knew it. Liam grins a lop-sided grin as he grabs a towel ready to head into the shower. After feeling all warm and fuzzy from cheering up the sweet stranded old lady, Liam couldn't just let me have my glory and win. Oh no, he then proceeded to collect another three numbers, completely shitting on my five.

'I'd rather it didn't if that's alright,' I say, feeling a little anxious about what's to come. 'I can't be scurrying around after you all night on my uni reunion. I need to be focusing on catching up with old friends, having fun and…'

'Making Brandon jealous,' he interrupts. 'I got you; I was just joking. Of course, this evening is all about you, Charlotte. I will be the one doing all of the scurrying.' He looks at me pointedly then slings the towel over his shoulder before sashaying into the bathroom to get ready. Whilst he's getting ready, I message Lydia and Kate to tell them that we'll be down shortly as we're just freshening up. They instantly reply with whooping voice notes and ten celebration emojis. They're still in the hotel and aren't looking to go anywhere else until a little later. There's no mention of Brandon so I still don't know if he's here or not. I'm now thinking it would be better if he wasn't. I'm not in the mood for drama or confrontation although it was initially what I wanted. I'm tired from the long journey and now I just want to unwind and cut loose. Liam comes out of the bathroom twenty minutes later washed, dressed and looking every bit the charming Irish man. I try to hide my gasp with a fake yawn that ends up sounding like a mooing cow. He makes a face.

'Sorry, very tired,' I say, waving away my weird noise. It's not often I see him all spruced up, he's usually in dirty work gear with paint and mud splats all over them. He's wearing simple denim jeans coupled with a black wool jumper, his light brown hair is slightly quaffed up a little and he's even wearing aftershave. He's trimmed his beard a little, too. I smile a tight-lipped smile to stop myself from grinning from ear to ear; he's made quite the effort.

'How do I look?' he asks, turning around slowly. He stands still and holds his arms out, looking at me for approval and if I didn't know him better, I'd say he looked a little vulnerable.

'You look perfectly acceptable for tonight's event.' I nod then give him a thumbs up. God, when did I get so stiff? I really need a drink.

We leave our hotel room and pad down to the hotel bar. The nervous butterflies begin to dance about in my stomach. What if Brandon's here? What if he's brought someone? As we approach the fancy bar, I spot my old uni crew gathered around a few tables, laughing and chatting. Liam places his arm around me and this time, I let it stay there.

Hall Four, where it all began. The chant we used to sing plays over and over in my head. How have I not seen most of these guys for ten years? We were so close. We studied together, partied together, in fact we did a lot of our firsts together and when we left, we promised to do a big meet up at least every year but that never happened or if it did, I didn't know about it. The most I've managed is a Facebook stalk from time to time, it's sad as we were all thick as thieves at one point.

Even from a distance they all look the same, just better dressed and in a slightly fancier location than the student bar. Kate and Lydia are sitting with a few other girls from our third-year student house and the rest of Hall Four are gathered either side. Ziggy and Paul are standing up, doubled over laughing, obviously finding something very funny. No one else seems to have brought partners; I know that Kate and Lydia were leaving the husbands at home but I thought at least a few others would bring partners. Ziggy's a successful music manager now apparently to a couple of really high profile bands but I'm not sure what Paul does.

My heart stops and I pull on Liam's hand to bring him swiftly behind a huge cheese plant which is one of many that are dotted about the bar. The bar is actually very swanky and goes more with the exterior of the hotel than the 1970s reception and bedrooms. A thought crosses my mind that there are actually a lot of plants in the hotel, especially the bar. I briefly wonder who supplies them. Liam immediately follows suit, squeezing my hand back as a sign of reassurance. We stay here, behind the huge cheese plant in the hope we won't be spotted yet.

He's here.

It's Brandon.

Everything moves in slow motion as the lads call out to Brandon. He approaches them with a big grin on his face and a pint in each hand, swaggering like he's never swaggered before. He's dressed in jeans and a checked shirt; it may have even been one that I bought for him. He still has that same beautiful smile and seemingly strong legs underneath those jeans. He places the beers on the table then puts a lazy arm each around Ziggy and Paul. He doesn't look very tanned, and on further inspection, he's lost a lot of weight and something about his face looks different. I'm surprised at the sight of him. He's still lovely though and my heart twangs. When Liam came back from travelling/charity work he looked as if he'd been away but Brandon just doesn't. He doesn't appear to be with anyone else either, no girlfriend in tow which is a plus, as I'm not sure how I'd cope with seeing that. I squeeze Liam's hand to let him know that it's okay to carry on and we leave our hiding spot. Taking a deep breath, I roll my shoulders back and shake my hair back into place.

'Fuck him. You look fucking sensational,' Liam whispers in my ear, and I giggle loudly at the tickle his breath has made on my neck and the sheer pleasure of being told that I look amazing. I'm not sure if it was planned but he says this at just the right time as Brandon looks at me. Ha. Take that for a slap in the face. I revel in the feeling of Brandon seeing that I'm with Liam. Now who's the one with big dick energy?

'LOTTIE! YOU'RE FINALLY HERE!' Kate screams, running over with her arms open wide as Lydia and a few of the other gang excitedly follow after her. I make a conscious effort not to look at Brandon, instead I bask in the glory of seeing all of my old uni mates, hugging them close. The last time we all hugged like this, we parted ways with high hopes and big dreams. Some of us have achieved those dreams and more such as Ziggy.

'Wow you haven't changed!' Kate says, as she gives me a hug. I've missed her and Lydia so much, we did everything together. Now *they* do everything together, houses, husbands and, more recently, babies.

'Yeah, how long has it been since we've seen you? We didn't know if you were ever going to arrive,' Lydia says, coming in for a hug. 'Must be coming on for seven years,' she continues, as she stands back to appraise me.

'God knows, too bloody long that's for sure,' I say, as Tasha, Sam and Olivia bundle me and we spend a few minutes shrieking and exchanging the usual pleasantries on each other's appearance and how we haven't changed. A couple of the other guys wave over at us but leave us girls to it.

'Hey everyone,' Liam says, with a little wave. Oh no in all the excitement of seeing all of my old friends, I've completely forgotten to introduce him.

'Guys, this is Liam,' I say, taking his hand again. 'My boyfriend.' I bite my lip and gaze up at him as he pulls me in close. Okay, so a bit dramatic of me but if you're going to do something then you may as well go all in. So far we're pretty good at faking it but he better not get any ideas. Kate and Lydia smile politely and say hello but their smiles look more like grimaces. The others don't even manage a hello, instead their mouths drop open and then there's an awkward silence.

'I thought it was the barman bringing you over,' Kate finally stage whispers, looking positively horrified.

'No, but I definitely know how to drink,' Liam jokes, and a few of the girls giggle but the atmosphere doesn't change and there's a nervous edge to their voices. Olivia, Sam and Tasha don't even try to look happy for me.

'But what about Brandon?' Olivia hisses in Kate's ear and Kate gives me a sympathetic smile.

'Oh, is he here?' I say, loudly. 'He left *me* about six months ago so…' I shrug as if it's nothing but really my whole world collapsed when he left. It was all planned and then he buggered off to *find himself*. I wonder if he found anyone else in the process.

'What? That's not what he said,' Olivia says. I notice

Tasha tug on her sleeve as if to tell her to stop. What has he been saying?

'Right.' I frown, not sure what all the awkward weirdness is about. 'Anyway, let's go and get a drink, we're very thirsty,' I say, as I turn to smile at Liam who I notice is looking over in Brandon's direction, his jaw clenched.

Liam and I head straight over to the bar after refusing offers of people trying to buy us drinks. I need a little time to digest the almost hostile response to my new *boyfriend*. Is it because no one else has bought their significant other? No. It was clear that they were very much invited.

'I'll get these. Are you okay?' Liam asks carefully, as we get out of earshot of the gang.

'Sort of, I'll be okay once I've faced him properly. Are you okay?' I touch his arm. It takes guts to come to something like this and immediately be judged just because of who he's with. Brandon and I aren't together but that doesn't stop the gang thinking that we should be and that this new guy has stolen me off him.

'Of course, I'm used to people taking an instant dislike to me.' He grins and gently nudges my arm but I know it's the opposite, people always love him. 'What do you want to drink?' he asks.

'Just a coke will be great.' I need a clear head for this.

'Grand.' Liam nods and the barman comes over to take our order. 'Don't panic,' Liam says slowly, as we watch the barman. 'But we haven't discussed our backstory. I thought we better get on the same page about that, just in case we're asked,' he continues, and I feel my nostrils begin to flare.

'Oh fucculent.' I fan my face with both hands, doing the exact opposite of what he's just told me to do.

'It's fine, relax.' Liam's eyes crinkle up then the rest of his face breaks out into a smile which instantly makes me feel better. 'You're quite cute when you're all flustered.'

'I'm not flustered,' I say, tempted to call out to the barman to tell him to add Vodka to my coke, I don't and instead turn to face Liam. 'Right so we re-connected a couple of months ago when you came back from Thailand. You realised you've always loved me and you were just waiting in the wings the entire time. You asked me out on a date when you saw I was single, I said yes. That one date turned into a handful of dates and now we're an item and completely in love.' I stare at him pointedly.

'What?' he laughs. 'That's a bit strong, I'm not going to be telling people that. You make me sound like a complete sap, pathetic even.' His eyebrows move closer together enhancing his intense eyes even further. He watches me with amusement.

'How so?' I *raise* my eyebrows. How rude and as if the idea of being in love with me is so ridiculous. 'If you can't play along and make it believable then you shouldn't have offered to come.' I fold my arms and face the other way.

'There's no need for that now, I'll go along with it but leave out the always waiting in the wings lovey dovey soppy part.'

'Okay fine,' I agree, as the barman brings us our drinks.

'So, are you ready to go over?' Liam asks, after taking a sip of his cocktail, his drink choice took me by surprise, he ordered a Strawberry Daiquiri. I can't help but smile as he peers at me through the arrangement of umbrellas and fruit. I'm sure the barman went overboard on purpose. I take a large slurp of my coke.

'Let's do this.'

We walk over to the gang to hear them reminiscing about uni days and the impressive number of times that Kate ended up in the gossip column of the student magazine. She once stripped naked in the student union bar and got up on stage to announce this was now her new normal. Clothes were restricting her and she shouldn't be judged for wanting to be her natural self. That was until the bouncers dragged her off and sent her packing in an enormous hi-vis coat. She got her bottle of wine from the guy that dared her to do it and was back next week, fully clothed. Although actually come to think of it, I think that may have been me that time?! Shit.

We stand around the edge listening and laughing. Kate catches my eye but then Ziggy comes swaggering over before I can get to her.

'Lottie, how's it going?' he asks, slicking back his hair. He's everything I expect a music manager to look like; cool clothes, long hair and designer glasses. He was always dressed like that at uni, except that the glasses were cheaper. Ziggy has a confidence and an assurance about him that you can just tell he was born with. He's a natural born leader and was always destined to be successful at whatever he turned his mind to. He's also a songwriter in his own right and has already had two songs bought by a couple of successful vocal artists. You'd be tempted to hate him for it except that he's a really nice guy.

'Good thanks, Ziggy. How's things with you? This is Liam by the way, my boyfriend.'

'Nice one, good to meet you mate,' Ziggy says, shaking Liam's hand and then turning his attention back to me. He's polite to Liam but not his usual engaging and welcoming self. I guess his loyalties lie with Brandon.

'So, what's been happening with you girl? Did you stay in the scene or make a run for it?'

'I made a run for it, Zig. You know it wasn't for me plus it wouldn't have been fair to pursue something I wasn't that passionate about. I got an ordinary job as a P.A, did that for a few years but now I'm helping to run my friend's plant shop and absolutely loving it.' I grin a genuine big smile, leaving out the part-time bit. It's true I am so much happier since working with Willow. It's nothing to be ashamed of, it never was.

'Yeah? Good for you,' Ziggy says, then glances at Liam, the elephant in the room.

'Yeah, I help out a lot with the social media aspect of it which I really enjoy and it helps bring in more sales,' I find myself saying. I do really enjoy it there. A sudden wave of dread washes over me. What job will I do next? Willow doesn't need me full-time and my savings are running low. *Don't think about that now*, I tell myself. Priorities. Catch up with old friends. Make Brandon jealous. 'Liam's done a lot for charity work, haven't you, my lucky potato farm?' I outwardly wince at my new nickname for him, lucky potato farm? Seriously. I hold my breath, waiting for the PC police to perform a citizen's arrest on me at any second and rightly so. Liam lets out a snort beside me.

'Ah to be sure, to be sure,' he jokes and Ziggy chucks his head back and laughs. In my peripheral vision Brandon glares at us from between the two cheese plants.

He's fuming.

My plan is working.

Chapter 15

'Lottie, I've missed you.' Brandon, who's somehow managed to teleport over to us, has now launched himself towards me, forcing my arms into a long embrace. I inhale his minty smell and close my eyes. This is exactly what I wanted but it doesn't *feel* completely how I expected. Like a drug, bringing Liam seems to have worked a treat. This is the perfect outcome, right? 'You look gorgeous, lost a bit of junk in the trunk? Not much of a pudding now, we'll have to come up with a new nickname.' He pats my hips then pulls away from me before attempting to twizzle me round, a thing we used to do when we were a couple. A thing that I *don't* want to do right now. Not in front of everyone after six months of radio silence.

'Wow, what a fucking compliment,' Liam mutters and my mouth drops open.

'Alright mate,' Brandon says as his eyes move towards Liam, puffing his chest out. 'Well, I'm not going to take *you* seriously with your poncy girl's drink.' Brandon scoffs then flicks the end of Liam's straw, reminding me of a little, bratty kid.

'Why do you think it's alright to comment on the size of a woman's body?' Liam retorts, his Irish accent sounding stronger than ever.

'Sorry, but what has any of this got to do with you? Why are you even here?' Brandon attempts to take my hand again and I bat it away. 'What? Don't tell me you're together? Well well well...' he continues.

Liam clenches his jaw slowly and steps towards Brandon.

'Okkkaaayyy, this is all getting a bit tense, how about we all get a shot of something to chill everyone out. Limoncello?' Ziggy suggests. 'It's Liam, isn't it? Come with me, dude. I'm happy to treat everyone to some champagne too, if that's what people are into.' Ziggy tries but no one acknowledges him. Liam and Brandon glare at each other, now both with clenched jaws whilst I stand in between them like a helpless damsel in distress. This is what I wanted, right?

'I'd like to speak with Lottie alone,' Brandon says evenly.

'Come on mate, let's get a drink, I want to hear more about your charity work.' Ziggy takes Liam by the arm but he shrugs him off.

'Is that what you really want?' Liam asks, as he tenderly touches my cheek then tucks a stray curl behind my ear. The question feels loaded, either that, or he's very good at playing the boyfriend. Too good.

'Yes,' I say, blinking back a determined tear. 'I need to.'

Liam allows Ziggy to lead him over to the bar, he glances back a couple of times. The last time he mouths, *'Are you okay?'* I mouth back *yeah don't worry* then turn my attention back to Brandon who quickly rearranges his expression from twisty jealous face to puppy dog eyes and beautiful smile. I should be melting at that smile but it definitely looks different, bigger teeth? Whiter? I imagined that I would be delirious after not seeing him in the flesh for six months. It's really all I've thought about and pined for. An all-consuming obsession to see him again. To get him back, my boyfriend of ten years. My soulmate. Drinking partner in crime. I narrow my eyes, are those scabs on his head?

'Did you get my emails?' he asks, treating me to another boyish grin. He bites his lip in an attempt to look coy but it just looks a little like he's trying to get a bit of loose skin off.

'Yes, I got them. What made you include me in the round robin?' I mutter.

'Wanted to keep you in the loop, didn't I?' He takes both my hands and I feel a sadness come over me.

'You could have emailed me personally or rang me.' I look at my feet, desperately trying to blink back the tears.

'I was off grid,' he protests. 'I didn't really use a phone when I was travelling.'

'You left and then chucked me out of the house. Our house.' I flinch, kicking myself for not taking more of what was mine. You can accumulate a lot in ten years and apart from my personal belongings, clothes and a couple of pieces of furniture, I left everything else there. I didn't want to be around all of *our* stuff and looking back, I think I was hoping that when we got back together, I'd get my stuff back.

'I know, my parents can be dicks,' he almost sings. 'But Lottie, our relationship didn't end, it was just on a bit of a time out.' He looks at me pleadingly before continuing. 'But I see you've moved on with *him*,' he says, in a slightly bitter tone. I think about that for a second and try to remember when we discussed it being a time out. We didn't discuss that we broke up either but from his actions I thought it was pretty clear.

'Brandon, you told me you were going on a six-month holiday to find yourself; I'd say that's code for goodbye, we aren't together anymore, wouldn't you?'

Brandon frowns and shakes his head. 'You see that's the thing with us, communication was always lacking, wasn't it? But I've had time to do a lot of thinking and we just need to work on that a bit more and we'll be fine.' The non-homeless man complaining about women always assuming things, rings in my ears but there's assuming and then there's reading between the lines. This is the latter.

'Yeah?' I frown, I always thought I was a good communicator.

'We need to tell each other how we feel about certain things. Like I'll tell you if I think you're not pulling your weight around the house and you tell me if if if...' he says.

'You can't think of anything can you?'

'Not really, but I'm sure you can.'

'If you've been working on yourself like you say you have, surely you'd know what one of your weaknesses is.'

'Sure, I'm the worst neat freak there is. Guilty.' He holds both hands up and I want to slap him. I bet he's had all the girls swooning over his impressive dishwashing skills.

'Is that all you can come up with? Seriously?'

'What do you want me to say? I'm not going to hate on myself, that's another thing I've learnt whilst travelling, we need to be kinder to ourselves. Cut ourselves some slack from time to time, you know?' He sneers before a sly belch escapes his mouth and he giggles at the stinky burp surprise. He's a bit drunk and it makes me curl my lip at him. He couldn't even be sober on our first meeting after six months.

'What?'

'You're drunk.'

'So, I've had a few sherbets. So what? It's our uni reunion with the gang. Back where we belong after taking a break. A long break as far as they're concerned.' He chucks a thumb their way then continues to pollute the air with his words. 'Did you see how fat Lydia's got? Right porker. But she has had a couple of kids I guess, but still, you'd think she'd make an effort for her husband.' He presses his lips together and closes his eyes briefly, he's more drunk than I thought and he's gossiping about our sweet friend, *my* sweet friend.

It's ugly.

He's being ugly. 'Also, Ziggy is such a bore,' he says, faking a yawn which then turns into a real yawn. 'All he wants to talk about is work, work, work. Yeah, alright mate, we all know you kiss the actually talented people's arses so that you can make loads of money out of exploiting them. Fucking bore, Lottie. I don't go on about what I do and my job is *way* more interesting. I work in show biz too, for fuck's sake, I basically brush shoulders with Harry Styles.' He wiggles his hands to reference jazz hands but he hasn't finished. 'And Kate, she's got so grey, has anyone told her about hair dye? Kate and Lydia look way older than thirty-one, don't they? A couple of old Scottish hens, bet you're glad we didn't bother with them for all these years, you may have ended up just like them.'

'What? Happy?' I say, quietly.

'Oh come on, they're not happy. They're content maybe, but there's a difference.'

'And what's that?'

'We were happy and I realise that now.' He takes both my hands in his again. 'Lottie,' he says, as he lets go of one of my hands to shuffle around in his pocket. 'Here, is a symbol of my love.' By now everyone has gathered around us, the whole gang. Everyone he has slagged off. Furtively, I look for Liam but he's nowhere to be seen. Brandon looks down at me, a smile like a charming prince but he isn't charming at all. He's vile and how am I only just seeing this now? Or has he become worse in his efforts to find himself? If that's the case, what he found was a complete wanker. We used to enjoy a bitch and a laugh together. Always asking each other 'What's your goss?' but now it just feels wrong. It's sobering.

It's awful. Was I just as awful? Perhaps a little. I think of Kathy who I judged from the off, I thought she was a total dweeb but she's actually a decent person, a kind person. Also, these are my friends, the friends he always put off visiting for years, kept me away from, even. There's only one person he loves and that's himself.

I see that now.

'Don't panic, I'm not asking you to marry me, although maybe that's what you want,' he says, with a little lopsided grin that he probably thinks makes him look sexy but makes him look more like an injured rat. 'It's an eternity ring, because I really do want us to be together forever.'

I stare at the nauseating turquoise swirls embedded in a sand-coloured stone as he slips the ring onto my finger.

'It's an opal fossil, sourced from the deepest, darkest parts of the Australian outback. I was told by an elder Aboriginal than this rock is over five million years old. About when the dinosaurs roamed the earth. The gold ring was made by one of the Maharaja in India. Ring making is his hobby and I watched him make it, so it's pretty fucking special. Just like us.'

The whole gang hold their breath as I twizzle the ring around on my finger, gently pulling at it until it completely comes off and I let it fall onto the floor. The gang gasps. Brandon drops to his knees to pick it up and I fight the urge to say *while you're down there*. A phrase he so often loved to use and thought was hilarious whenever I bent down.

'I only wear silver. I'm allergic to gold. You should have remembered that.' I give the ring a little kick with the end of my shoe which sends it catapulting up into the air. Brandon's mouth hangs open as the ring heads for his front teeth and I wince as it makes a loud clunking sound when the ring meets the enamel, or should I say veneer.

'You bitch, I've only just had these done,' he whines, then holds his hand up to his mouth to cover up any damage. I think I've chipped it.

'By the way,' Brandon spits through his fingers. 'Mum and Dad didn't want you out of the house, it was me.' He gives me one more disparaging look then scuttles off back out of my life. . . again.

Chapter 16

The round of applause and cheers take me by surprise.
Then the gang start with the old Hall four chant:
Hall four, hall four
Move out of my way
Hall four, hall four
We're here to play
Hall four, hall four
Don't hate, just cheer.
Hall four, hall four
Let's go, more beer.

Limbs wrap themselves around me and I'm encased
in the old gang hall four embrace, the inevitable bundle
every time someone triumphs or commiserates. It feels
so good, it's so nice to be supported by the old gang. It
takes me a moment to realise that they've *all* sided with
me. Not one of them has gone after Brandon, even Ziggy
is still here. Despite myself I feel a pang of empathy for
him. No one should be on their own.

'That was amazing!' Kate says, in a hysterical tone as
Lydia jumps up and down beside her.

'So brilliant! You showed that pig!' Lydia says.

'Who does he think he is?' Kate says, before putting
on a voice, 'Sourced from the deepest, darkest parts of

the Australian outback.' Everyone laughs. 'As if that was going to win you over. I'm proud of you, babe.' Kate comes in for another hug and I squeeze her back, tears pricking at my eyes.

'He is a pig.' I sniff. 'Of the highest order.' I begin to well up again and through blurred vision I see everyone's faces change from excitement to concern. I quickly blink the tears back, I won't let *him* ruin this reunion. It's not going to be all about him.

'Fuck him,' I say, rising from the gallows and drying my eyes. 'Let's get drunk, hall four style.' I fling my arms up into the air, suddenly feeling like I've just won the *X Factor*. Liam's friendly face comes into view and I'm so pleased to see him that I clasp his beard in my hands as the gang cheer once more. Egged on by the hysteria, I bring his lips to mine and give him a spine-tingling kiss that oddly makes me feel as if I'm levitating. The noise fades away as Liam's hands travel up my body and our tongues entwine even further. It's probably the hysteria and the ambience but this kiss is on fire. I now know what all the romance novels mean when they describe an electrifying kiss.

They mean this.

'Do you want a drink?' Liam asks in a gruff tone, as he pulls away from me. He searches my eyes and I fight the urge to kiss him again. The crowd begin to mumble and disperse as a few other guys from uni arrive, leaving only Kate and Lydia with us.

'Sure, I'd love one,' I squeak, as the girls wait with baited breath beside me.

'Same again?' he asks with a kind smile and I give him

the thumbs up. As hard as it is not drinking alcohol with my uni mates, it's actually probably a good idea to stay on the cokes, with all the high emotions I just know I'd do something I'd regret if I got too drunk. I was always a bit of a liability in that way.

'Girls? Drink?' He looks to Kate and Lydia who visibly swoon in his presence.

'Oh thank you, um, wine for us please,' Kate answers.

'Yes, white please, Liam,'

'Lottie are you not going to join us in the wine?' Lydia asks as I shake my head and wave my hand. 'Not for me thanks.' Kate and Lydia exchange a weird look, are they on to us?

We all watch him walk off to the bar in silence.

'Well, well, well,' Kate says. 'That was like something off a film, you've certainly found yourself a keeper there.'

'Yeah, it's just that…' I'm just about to come clean and confess that Liam is in fact my fake boyfriend, when Lydia interrupts.

'He's truly gorgeous, where did you meet again?'

'He's my brother's friend, I've known him for years, we just hadn't really talked much as adults what with me being with Brandon and everything.'

'You've certainly upgraded there,' says Kate, as she nods towards Brandon who's chatting up some girl in the corner of the bar. I watch him slide his hand into his pocket, leaning more on one leg than the other as he smooths his other hand through his hair. Well, he didn't waste any time. The pretty blonde girl giggles at something he's said and I feel sorry for her. Don't fall for it, I want to yell. I did ten years and all I got was a lousy ring that meant nothing. A ring that wasn't to my taste at all. He didn't know me. Did he ever? Was I ever the real me when I was with him? I've changed so much over the last few months.

'Forget him,' Kate continues. 'He's only doing that to try and piss you off and you've moved onwards and upwards to the dreamboat that is Liam.'

'Yes, yes I have,' I lie, as I watch Liam have a laugh with the barman. He's such good fun. Brandon was always a mean drunk and I wasn't much better, come to think of it. 'Let's finish these drinks and go somewhere a bit more low key,' I say, as I spy Brandon who's now laughing with a different girl. Both of them are sucking on lemons, with shot glasses in their hands. I can see his chipped tooth from here but he clearly isn't bothered, or maybe he's forgotten. 'I've had enough drama for one night,' I say as Liam pats my leg which makes me feel hyper aware of my body.

An hour later and after hearing about Kate's new business venture as a virtual HR assistant and Lydia's naughty child who painted her little friend's eyes with nail varnish, we leave. Luckily it was kid friendly so it peeled off but Lydia said her heart was in her mouth when she saw her. 'I imagined the kid going blind and Evie having to go to some sort of child prison.'

We're out on Deansgate Locks. Kate recommends a little underground bar called The Locomotive so we go there. It's dark with lanterns scattered around and lots of little steps leading to cosy cubby holes. It's hard not to trip down the shallow steps and I cling onto Liam's arm for support. He gives me a sideways glance followed by a smirk.

'I'll fall to my death if I don't have something to cling to. I need you as my anchor,' I whisper, as Kate and Lydia trot down the stairs arm in arm in front of us.

'Don't worry, this ship hasn't sailed yet,' he teases, as I dig him in the ribs then nearly lose my footing in the process. He catches me as I catch my breath. I'll tell the girls the story behind me and Liam in a bit. I'll tell them the truth.

After revisiting the details of Brandon's weird non-proposal, the girls piss themselves laughing at me damaging his new, bright white veneers that I've since found out he got done in Turkey. Brandon's new Turkey teeth were the height of discussion moments before I arrived, that and his hair transplant, which I didn't even notice or think he needed. Come to think of it, his hair did look different. Perhaps he was wearing a wig to cover it up but I could still see the scabs. Rather than finding himself, he was reinventing his looks more like which isn't a bad thing I guess because whatever makes you happy and all that but Turkey teeth? They were near enough glow in the dark. We're now on our third round of drinks, sipping out of old jam jars.

'I'm sure this one wasn't a jam jar,' I say, turning it around in my hand. 'It looks more like a mayonnaise jar or a pickle jar,' I continue, scratching at the label that hasn't been fully washed off.

'I bet you wished it was pickled gherkins though.' Liam laughs.

'No way, not mixed in with a pina colada mocktail, that's revolting,' I say, pulling a face.

'Do you still eat them, Lottie?' Lydia asks. 'I thought it was a poor person uni snack.'

'No, it's just a poor Lottie thing,' I joke. 'I'm addicted, always have been. They're just so moorish,' I say, as my mouth involuntary salivates.

'It's probably a bit of an addiction but one I'm not willing to give up just yet.'

'She's lucky I like them, or I'd make her brush her teeth before she kisses me every time,' Liam jokes, as his hand rests on my thigh. It feels so intimate, so real. Now isn't really the right time to tell them we aren't actually together. It would open up a whole can of worms and I'm too embarrassed to explain, plus I'm enjoying it all a little too much.

'I wish I had someone that loved me like that,' Lydia blurts out, as she looks down at her empty jam jar.

'You do,' Kate says, putting an arm around Lydia. 'Marriage is just hard work, it's easy in the early days of a relationship, all exciting sex and cooking for each other. No clearing up other people's shit and discovering nasty habits, that comes a least a year later if not longer. No offence guys,' Kate says to Liam and I.

'Oh no offence taken,' Liam says, holding his hands up.

'He's left me,' Lydia blurts out, and we all gasp.

'What? No. He hasn't!' Kate gasps as her hand flies up to her cheek.

'I'm afraid he has, just before the reunion, he's met someone from work.'

'Oh Lydia, I'm so sorry,' I say.

'Why didn't you say before?' Kate asks. 'You've been carrying this round with you the whole time?'

'I know, I wanted to enjoy the reunion, plus I was embarrassed everyone is doing so well with their new ventures and successful relationships that I didn't want to be the big bad failure in the room.'

'Oh Lydia,' we all say in unison, as Kate and I each put an arm around her. Looks like I wasn't the only one feeling that way.

'Yes. I failed at marriage at the age of thirty-one.'

'It happens to the best of us, don't be hard on yourself, Lydia,' Liam pipes up and I resist the urge to ask him if he was ever married. I don't think he was but who knows. His comment makes me wonder and he did say he had some stuff to sort out when he returned from his travels.

'Does it? I just feel like I wasn't good enough to keep him. I've had his children and now I'm overweight and overtired. I neglected him and now he's gone elsewhere. I don't blame him.' She sniffs as Kate and I rub an arm each.

'You're gorgeous! Truly,' Liam pipes up. 'He's a selfish bastard and he should have treated you better. See that guy over there,' Liam continues, pointing to a man with lots of hair and a checked shirt. 'He's been checking you out since we walked in. You've still got it and from what I can tell you're a lovely person with a grand sense of humour. I certainly would if I wasn't already betrothed to this formidable woman.' I giggle at Liam's choice of words and wonder who this man is who's saying all the right things. The piss taker is now the kind gentleman and it's wildly attractive. Calm yourself, Lottie. The jam jar sugary mocktail is going to your head, it must be laced with something else. A hallucinogenic, yes that must be it.

'Thanks,' Lydia says, as Kate hands her a tissue from her handbag.

'He went off with some woman from his work,' she continues. 'Ten years younger and a body like Kim Kardashian. I found the *Facebook* messages on our laptop when he was out one night.' Lydia shakes her head and honks her nose loudly.

'So sorry mate, what a shit.' I shake my head in disbelief.

'He doesn't deserve you, mate,' Kate says. 'I can't believe it. Paul will punch him when he finds out.'

'I hope so.' Lydia manages a small giggle.

'You'll get there, Lyds. I was with Brandon for the best part of ten years but today I looked at him and genuinely felt nothing. I'm over him.' Am I over him?

'Yeah, it helps that you had someone dishy to get under though,' Lydia says, nodding in the direction of Liam.

Liam gives her a charming smile and brushes some non-existent dust off his shoulder.

'How did you guys end up getting together?' Kate asks, as she grins at Liam and I.

'Oh, umm it was, we were…' I begin, completely forgetting what story we agreed on.

'I'm friends with her brother, have been since we were kids. I'd always thought she was amazing. Always admired her from afar.'

I smile. He's going with my story, after all his complaining.

'The way she shakes those ringlets into place, throws her head back when she laughs and isn't afraid to say when something isn't right have always had me transfixed, even as a young boy,' Liam continues, as Kate and Lydia swoon. 'To be honest, I always thought she was way out of my league. I used to tease her a lot as a kid and I could tell she despised me for it but I was a teenage dickhead incapable of communication with girls, especially pretty ones.'

'Didn't despise him.' I shake my head, smirking. 'Just thought he was an idiot.'

'And I was, a fool. A complete fool for you.'

'Oh stop,' I say, patting him on the arm, giggling. He takes my hand in his and kisses it gently and sensuously. I try hard not to let a groan escape me. Who is this man and what have they done with Liam?

'So, how did you get from that to this?' Lydia asks

impatiently, gesticulating at us, not missing a beat. Liam rests his hand on his knee with mine still entwined in his. I squeeze it, but it's more a warning than anything else. Please don't make up anything too soppy or weird. If we have to keep lying to my friends, then keep it classy at least.

'Well,' Liam starts, before eyeing me shyly. He's a good actor, I'll give him that. 'I came back from Thailand and after having witnessed a few things out there, I decided life's too short. There's no time for what ifs, you've only got one life so if you want something then go for it.'

'Ohhh, what happened in Thailand?'

'Kate!' Lydia admonishes, 'he might not want to talk about it.'

'No, it's fine. Out there, the kids I was working with have nothing. But when I say nothing I mean materialistic stuff but their hearts are so full and they are so grateful for each other and anything that they do get. They're positive and upbeat almost all the time, they make the most of what they've got.'

'Okay but what happened?' Kate pushes.

'The grandfather of a little boy that I taught passed away, well he was on death's door when I got there. He was seen as the village mentor but had been ill for quite some time. The little boy took me to meet him a few times before he died and the last time I saw him he said that there were three things to live by.'

'What are they?' Kate asks, she's fully invested but I'm equally as curious.

'Be kind to yourself, be kind to others and always do the thing you're most scared of doing.'

'Awww, your biggest thing was telling Lottie how you really felt?' Lydia swoons and I lean into Liam, giving him a quick dig in the ribs. He's taken it a bit too far.

'It was *the biggest* thing I was scared of doing.' He's taking the piss now. I glance at his face which is arranged in a modest, slightly shy expression. His face looks slightly pink, although that could be the fairy lights dangling above his head reflecting back onto his skin. I don't know how I feel about fairy lights outside of Christmas time, it kind of looks like they've forgotten to take down the decorations.

'That's so lovely, you're both very lucky to have found each other,' Lydia says. 'It gives me hope, anyway.'

I smile at Lydia feeling extremely guilty for lying to one of my oldest, best friends. I've sold her a dream that simply isn't true and not only that, she believes that she can have it too.

The truth is, all men are shits and I'm going to hell for this.

Chapter 17

'Here's your breakfast your highness,' I say, as I slide the bacon sandwich onto the table. I finish making two cups of tea and place them on the table too.

'Could I have some tomato ketchup please?' a smug faced Liam asks. 'Bit dry without any sauce,' he explains, with a grimace.

'Of course.' I grab the ketchup out of the fridge along with the brown sauce and mayonnaise. Well, if I'm going to be the slave for seventy-two hours then I may as well do it properly and offer him a selection of sauces.

'Oh, there's a problem.'

'There is? What could one possibly want now?' The seventy-two hours only started when we got back from Manchester yesterday afternoon and so far he's had me make him dinner. Well, it was for Harry and Kathy as well, I made lovely chicken and leek pie with dauphinoise potatoes and it was delicious, even if I do say so myself. Kathy screamed with hysterics when we told them about Del Boy from *Only Fools and Horses* turning up as my escort, at least I've come clean about that now. Harry just called me unhinged and said I should be using my savings to save for a deposit for a place to live and not on gigolos masquerading as chaperones. I near enough died right there and then on the spot but I guess he does have a point. What on earth was I thinking? And all it's done is force me into a web of lies. A web of lies that I'll have to keep up because I've agreed to invite the girls down for the weekend once I, I mean *we,* are settled in our new place.

'Sauces like this, should not be kept in the fridge. They cool down the bacon too quickly making the sandwich cold.' His mischievous blue eyes watch me from above his bacon sandwich. He's an awfully picky master.

'Okay, well, there's nothing I can do about that right…'

'I'd like you to warm each bottle of sauce underneath your armpit until it's room temperature,' he says, not taking his eyes off me. 'Well, go on then…' He nods at the bottles placed in front of him on the table.

I tell my face not to react then lean over and grab a sauce bottle in each hand. I whip the mayonnaise and brown sauce underneath my armpits then without hesitation, put the tomato ketchup in between my legs. I'm wearing a long skirt and the ketchup feels cold even through my tights. Liam's chuckling slowly turns to him sitting there with his mouth hanging open. Hah! He wasn't expecting that, was he?

We spend the next few minutes staring at each other whilst I wait for the sauce to heat up to body temperature. I watch him bite his lip in enjoyment and I grin back at him. If I show him that none of this shit phases me, he's surely going to lay off a bit. I'm doing reverse psychology on him. Or at least I think I am. The armpit sauces appear to be ready first so I shuffle and place them down on the table. Liam just sits there and licks his lips. He's waiting for the ketchup of course, that's what he asked for. I shimmy round to his side of the table, hoist myself up onto the table then flick open the bottle with my finger then squeeze the sauce out with my thighs, all onto his bacon sandwich. It covers half the table too and I get a bit on his hands and mine. But this is what he wanted, right? I lick my fingers seductively, wincing at the sharpness of the sauce as I watch him take his first bite.

'Oh good God, what's going on here?' Kathy squeals from the kitchen doorway. 'Is this that weird food porn that everyone's into at the moment? What's it's called? Sploshing?'

'I don't know what's worse.' Willow laughs after having spent an hour having her ear bent about my reunion and escort escapades and the seventy-two-hour slavery that I'm now subjected too. At least I'm at work so can avoid any slave tasks for a good seven hours now. 'The fact you nearly took an extra from *lock stock and two smoking barrels* on the uni reunion or Kathy walking in on you and Liam getting intimate.' Willow screams with laughter as I cringe and bite into my gherkin.

She turns on the sprinklers for the living wall, wafting the spray towards her face to cool and calm her down. She's been installing the wall all weekend to showcase how lovely it can look and it looks just that. Big Boston ferns drape across one side as prayer plants creep through the middle, showcasing their beautiful painted leaves. A hint of romantic ivy trails down the other side, balancing it out just perfectly. The next job will be to film it and make some promo videos for social media. I can't wait to get started. My stomach drops as I think of the possibility of another plant shop opening in the town but I have a few ideas up my sleeve. I still haven't told her about it and that reminds me, I need to try and find a way to speak to Mr Woodling. I don't want to tell Willow my plan just yet, plus she's only back for a few days and then she's going to see her mum again. Things aren't looking good. She really doesn't need the extra stress, what with her mum being so ill.

'It wasn't intimate,' I say, indignantly.

'Well, what was it then? You were squeezing sauce onto his bacon sandwich with your bloody thighs, woman.'

'My thighs weren't bloody, it was the ketchup,' I quip.

'You know what I mean.'

'Sadly, I do. Oh what a sight that must have been for poor Kathy's eyes. She'll never look at me the same way again. It must have looked like something out of a horror movie.'

'Sounds to me like she was excited, this sploshing that everyone talks about?' Willow teases.

'Oh yuk, don't!'

'Bet she has a right old time with your brother and her iced buns!' Willow guffaws.

'No! Stop!' I scream but I'm glad I've given her a laugh. I've missed my workmate. 'I don't want to think about her iced buns or anyone else's for that matter.'

'Did someone say iced buns?' Malcolm appears grinning with a paper bag in each hand as if summoned by the pastry gods.

'Oh hey, Malc, how are you?' Willow says, still tending to her living wall.

'Yes, yes, good, good, can't complain.' Malcolm looks between Willow and I furtively as he shifts on his feet. 'Lovely arrangement,' he says, eyeing the living wall display as he hands each of us a brown bag with a tasty treat inside. The smell is sickly sweet and my stomach rumbles for whatever's inside.

'Why, thank you Malc.' Willow smiles.

'These are my secret family recipe iced buns, you'll never taste another bun quite like it.

'Oh right, I can't wait,' I say, as I open up the bag and inhale the delicious, freshly baked smell. Even after a pickled gherkin I could still smash down one of Malcolm's treats. Gherkins are like a pallet cleanser to me anyway, as strange as that sounds.

'I love a good bun.' Willow winks at me and I try not to smirk.

'Well,' Malcolm whispers, leaning in closer. 'You may like buns but I don't suppose you'd like a bun fight?'

'Umm probably not,' I say, wondering how much we'll have to beg today to get the cryptic message out of Malcolm. 'Yes, no one really likes confrontation, do they?' I add.

'Oooh, I don't know, I quite enjoy it sometimes,' Willow muses. 'If I know I'm right of course, it's quite enjoyable watching someone squirm as you put them in their place.'

'Doesn't sound like you Willow?' I study my friend who now has a pained expression on her face. She's usually as zen as you like.

'No, it doesn't, does it?' she says in a deepened tone. 'But all that driving I've been doing back and forth to Mum and Dad's has made me see what utter wankers there are on the road. I lost my shit a few times and I felt so much better afterwards for letting it out.'

'Yes,' Malcolm says, pulling a face at Willow's potty mouth. 'Sometimes things are better out in the open aren't they?' Oh no. He's going to tell her about the plant shop. He's going to tell her about the plant shop. Nooo.

'Oh for goodness' sake, Malcolm just spit it out,' Willow snaps, as Malcolm and I exchange shocked expressions. 'Sorry, but I've got no time for this, my mum is at death's door in a hospice so if you have something to tell us then please just be frank for once. We love your treats, they're very nice indeed and we appreciate them but please just cut the crap for once.'

'Well, okay then.' Malcolm bristles slightly, straightening his white baker's jacket. 'If you put it like that, I'll be frank. Mr Woodling wants your shop.'

'What do you mean, he *wants* my shop?'

'He had plans to open up a plant shop in the new premises up the road but now that's fallen through and he's very keen on your space.'

'Well, he can be as keen as he likes, he isn't getting my shop. It's mine.'

'No? Not even if he offers the landlord more money? We could all do with more money these days…'

'No. My landlord simply wouldn't do that. He's a decent guy,' Willow says, but I'm not sure how much of that is true. I seem to remember her saying that the landlord lives abroad and she doesn't have much to do with him apart from pay the rent. If that's true then Mr Woodling might stand a very good chance of tempting him with a better offer.

'Okay, just simply saying what I've heard on the grapevine.'

'Okay, thanks Malcolm, it's appreciated,' Willow says. 'Sorry I snapped.'

'It's not a problem and sorry about your mother.'

'Thanks, Malc.' Willow blinks back tears.

'Well, I think we're going to need some time to let this news sink in,' I say. 'Thanks for the treats, Malc, we'll give you some feedback next time you pop in.' I put my hand on the small of his back and gently begin to usher him out of the door. Customers have just come into the shop and the last thing we want is for them to hear any of Malcolm's gossip.

True or not.

Chapter 18

Taking my usual window seat on the bus, I reach into my handbag for my phone to pas the time. I end up scrolling on *Instagram* and snooping on the woman I aspire to be which is of course NextLevelNyssa. It's been a while since I've allowed myself to get lost in her world and dream of a more abundant, happier life. I haven't felt the need to snoop on her grid in a while because I think I'm getting there in my own way. I may not have all the things that a woman in her thirties feels she should have but I do feel much happier, lighter. I enjoy my work and the people I live with and since breaking up with Brandon, I genuinely feel like a kinder, nicer person.

I didn't realise I wasn't when I was with him but I'm definitely more kind. I feel a need to help people more than I ever did. My thoughts turn to the fake homeless man outside the shop and the little granny who wanted my brownie recipe. I've come a long way and since saying goodbye once and for all to Brandon, I feel a huge sense of relief and freedom. I wasted ten years with him and I'm not going to waste any more years on a man. The next person I choose to be with, if I choose to be with anyone, is going to have to be extra special. A catch.

Today's post finds NextlevelNyssa sitting crossed

legged on a beautiful beach with, her normally straight silky bob scooped up into a tiny little bun. I'm surprised to see that the underneath of her hair is shaved and on the nape of her neck is a tattoo in what looks like Hindi. Her hands are on her knees and her long index fingers elegantly touch her thumbs. There's a beam of white light above her head and I can't tell if it's been *Photoshopped* in or is just a photo taken at the right time to make her look like a living angel. Underneath her photo is the caption. *Live it, breath it, become it. Don't waste time with the people who bring you bad energy, you want that big love energy. You want people to raise your vibrations, not bring them down. The same goes for you, be a mood enhancer not a mood hoover. Straighten that crown and become the person you would look up to when you were a child. Be you, a kind version, and you'll be okay. I want you to say this out loud now, wherever you may be. 'I am releasing all negative emotions from my nervous system and I deserve a loving life.'*

I glance furtively around the bus to see if anyone would hear me, there's only the bus driver and an old couple sitting at the back of the bus. In front of me, a teenager with huge headphones is listening to music so loud that it's probably close to deafening him. As I gaze out of the window at the beautiful views of Coolsbay bay, I say the words quietly but with conviction.

'I am releasing all negative emotions from my nervous system and I deserve a loving life.'

'Yes, you do my lovely, yes you do.' Rupert, the bus driver nods at me via his mirror and offers a smile.

Smiling back at him, I stare out of the window for a few moments before going back to my phone. I unfriend Brandon on Facebook then go and find his emails with the links to his monthly travel blog, I delete all of them, every single one. It feels good. All traces of him gone.

His big dickhead energy, no more.

Bouncing through the front door, I get home, looking forward to a big hot bubble bath and an early night. All this inner work I've just done on the bus has worn me out and I deserve a pampering.

'You're looking awfully happy today,' Liam says, as I glide into the living room.

'Yeah, you know, just loving life, appreciating the little things, I'm zen,' I say, with a little shrug before mimicking NextLevelNyssa's hand meditation positions.

'Grand, then you won't mind polishing my work boots for me and making my tea again tonight?'

'What?' Is he for real? He's so mean, I wouldn't be half as mean if I had won. The amount of cooking he has me doing is just ridiculous. He knows I *hate* cooking, baking is more my bag but even that I find tedious.

'A deal's a deal. Oh, and if you could run me a bath then that would also be awesome. My limbs are aching from all the painting I've been doing and…'

'Oh poor you,' I say, before looking at my watch. 'Thank God you only have twelve hours left of this deal, I can't stomach being your slave for much longer, it's torture. Not the chores as such just looking at your smug face,' I tease, suppressing a slight smirk myself.

'Oi slave, that is no way to talk to your master,' he croaks. 'I shall now demand a bath by candlelight and you can read to me.'

'Read to you? In the bath?' I ask, incredulous. He has some cheek.

'Yes, what a good idea. Don't worry I'll protect my modesty with bubbles and my hands.' He cups his hands and moves them onto his groin, the facial expression of a naughty school boy.

'You will not.'

'Or not?' He puts his hands up in the air.

'You'll wear your swim shorts if this is going to happen and before you suggest it, no way am I getting in the bath. What am I reading to you?' I fold my arms. He's pushing his luck.

'You're such a spoil sport,' he laughs. 'Okay, swim shorts it is.'

His lordship had chilli for dinner, which was a tad on the spicy side. I looked up the recipe online and we didn't have all of the ingredients so it was sort of improvised. I have to say, today I quite enjoyed being creative and chucking in the chilli, herbs and spices. We didn't have any kidney beans so I added in some baked beans and sweetcorn. I tasted it half way through and it tasted pretty good but then I got a little too confident and slap happy with the chilli. I didn't bother to taste it again but fussed around sorting out the rice, two pots of sour cream dip and of course the icing on the cake or should I say, the pièce de resistance – the pickled gherkin on the side. I chopped them up into tiny little pieces, hoping he wouldn't figure out my special ingredient straight away. You have to believe me. Gherkins go so well with a chilli and I didn't even know it myself until today. After a few coughs and splutters from Liam, he agreed that my chilli was edible and the gherkins definitely enhanced the meal by at least one star, giving it a whole two stars, the first star being for effort. Cheeky git. Harry and Kathy decided to go out for food, the decision was made when

Kathy saw me pouring in a whole tin of baked beans, the look of horror on her face was quite the picture. Well, I tried my best and even though it was a bit gross, I enjoyed the creative process.

Now, I'm running his bath. I gaze at the black and white tiled floor and watch the tiles morph into a wavy 3D hole. My stomach mimics the hallucination going on within my eyes. Am I nervous? No. It's just a bath and he'll be in his swim shorts. I'll be reading to him, like I'm his teacher or something, reading him an instruction manual on how to swim perhaps? Who am I kidding, knowing Liam, it will be something raunchy to embarrass me like *Fifty Shades of Grey*. He still hasn't told me what the book is, I didn't know he was even a reader.

I rummage around in the cupboards looking for his wash bag, which is almost the same size as my handbag and labelled LM in big white silky stitching. I pull out the purple wash bag and smile at the fact he's labelled it, perhaps he needed to when travelling, but I can't imagine taking this to hostels. It's huge. I pull out a large purple bubble bath soak for achy limbs and dollop a generous amount into the bath. The smell of lavender infiltrates my nostrils and I inhale deeply. I love that smell. I notice he has some foot rub in there too so I pull that out. This bath isn't going to phase me and if master wants a foot rub, then that is what he'll get. I set the scrub down at the end of the bath and snicker to myself at the glittery bath bomb that I've found. Oh well, full works and all that. I chuck that in too and watch the water fizz and pop before it changes colour to bright pink in between the bubbles.

To my amusement I spy a couple of facemasks for dry skin. I pull them out of the wash bag and decide I'll do one with him, my skin has got a bit dry this winter and it's in need of a good moisturise. I set them on the other side of the bath before hunting out the candles, dotting them around the bathroom and the windowsill. The bath looks so inviting and I'm so tired that a good soak would do me the world of good but it isn't for me. I decide I'll run a bath like this for myself tomorrow and I might ask to borrow his stuff as it's totally up my street, not his usual wood and cinnamon aroma but lovely all the same. He wanted a pretty bath bomb and he got one. Fair play. I stand back and admire the inviting, lush smelling, relaxing scene and decide that it is missing one thing. Music!

Sam Fender plays quietly in the background and as he sings about *Being able to talk to anyone but you,* I let a smile spread across my lips then almost shit my pants at the loud knock on the door.

'Can I come in?' Liam's Irish drawl comes from the other side of the door.

'You sure can,' I sing, before opening the door to Liam who's wearing a very short pair of pale pink shorts and carrying a book in his hand. This man loves pink. To be fair, they are quite mild compared to what I was expecting, which is Liam in a red thong. Expecting or was I hoping? I try my best not to focus on his toned torso and his perfectly formed arms. He's lost most of his tan now and his fair skin reminds me of a snowdrop.

'Wow, it smells like a whore's bedroom in here.' Liam laughs, albeit a little nervously as he enters the bathroom. My smile turns into a bemused look, but it's all your stuff. All your fancy whore stuff, I think.

'I mean, it's beautiful, the effort you've gone to is lovely,' he continues, hovering by the bath, staring at the glitter sparkling in the candlelight.

'I'm going to look like a sparkling unicorn when

you're done with me here.' He chuckles lightly.

'Yes, but a very nice smelling unicorn.' I hold my hand out to take the book from him; he hesitates then forces the dusty hardback with no cover into my hands.

'I'm intrigued.' I turn the book over in my hands; it looks ancient.

'Don't open it yet,' he says quickly. 'I'll get in first and enjoy the ambience.'

'Okay, squire.'

'Squire.' Liam laughs. 'I think you mean master.'

'I prefer squire.'

He lowers himself into the bath. 'Christ woman are you trying to boil me alive inside and out?' he shrieks, and I let out a high-pitched giggle that I didn't know I had in me.

'Too hot for your delicate skin?' I tease. 'Sorry, I'll add some cold, I just made it how I would have it. I like it hot, I guess.'

'First you try to kill me with the chilli and then this, you're lucky you're a sight for sore eyes, Grotty.'

'Oi, no Grotty anymore, remember.' Sight for sore eyes, hey? No one has ever described me as that before, is that even a compliment? It doesn't sound like one but the way that he's looking at me makes me think that perhaps it is.

'We're not in a fake relationship anymore, remember,' he says softly as he raises an eyebrow.

'No, we're not, but I'm not Grotty anymore, either.'

'Gotcha and I'm not an arsehole anymore.'

'Maybe.'

Chapter 19

The bath stool feels a little wobbly under my weight. I carefully cross my legs and hold my breath so as not to cause the thing to completely buckle beneath me and catapult me into the bath with Liam. Is that what I want? To be with Liam? Nope. It was a pretend relationship to show my ex that I was capable of attracting someone who loves me for me. Oh the irony. Brandon would be laughing through his chipped Turkey teeth if he knew the truth.

'You alright?' Liam's voice cuts through my thoughts. His face is faintly etched with something that resembles worry slash curiosity.

'Yes good,' I say breathlessly, trying my best to focus on the book and not Liam's toned shoulders and arms that are draped over the side of the bath. 'Right, let's get started.' I open the dusty book in the palm of my hands and read the words. 'Poems for you.' Before looking at Liam and frowning.

'Really, this is what you want me to read to you?' I didn't have him down as a poem kind of guy.

'Yes, why not,' he says, with a straight face.

I look down at the pages and begin to read about a little mouse named Ewan. Liam chuckles lightly as the amusing poem leaves my mouth, at one point he slaps the bath water and some of the water lands on my face, I stay in character as the mouse makes his escape, quickly wiping the water away as Liam continues to lap up the poem. Next, I try a tongue twister which looks easier on paper than it does to read out loud.

'You're a good narrator.' He smiles, his eyes glistening once I've finished the tongue twister.

'Why, thank you.' I grin back at him then look away, feeling awkward that he's looked at me too much. And, perhaps, me at him.

'Do you think you could skip to page forty-five and read that poem, it's a good one.'

'Sure.' I skip to the requested page then clear my throat.

'Hello little one, you're so pure and new.

There's no hint of judgement or resentment from you.

This life will be crazy and sometimes too much but don't worry, you'll be given the tools to cope and have hope that if you make a mistake, mess up and do wrong, it's okay.

I've got you little one.

You're learning, stay strong.

When you feel a bit scared that the world is too big and you are so small, what have you got to give?

Just remember you're special, loved and unique, there isn't a limit to how high you can peak.

And little one, please always know, that wherever you go, whatever you do, I will always, always be right here for you.'

I close the book. 'Well, that was a very sweet poem.' I glance at Liam to find that he has his eyes shut. During the poem, I was stealing looks at him and was surprised to see him reciting the poem with me at times.

Setting the book down on the corner of the bath, I slowly lean forward and splash his face with a bit of water. That'll wake him up. 'Oi, it's rude to sleep whilst someone reads to you.' I giggle as his eyes ping open and he looks at me with an expression that I don't recognise. I splash him again, this time, it's a much bigger splash and I accidently stroke his thigh and possibly something else. The water drenches his face but also the book that I'd placed on the side. Woops. He doesn't look pleased.

'Oh fuck.' Liam jumps up and rescues the book, he quickly flicks through the pages before blowing air out of his cheeks then rests it tentatively on the radiator. He stares at the book.

'I'm sorry,' I say quietly, tempted to put my hand on his still wet shoulder but instead I wring my hands. 'Is it all right?'

'Yeah, I'm sure it will be fine when it dries out.' He looks around for a towel and grabs the hand towel off the rail, quickly drying his body then hair, still looking at the book.

'Don't you want me to get you a proper towel?' I ask, puzzled by his strange change in mood.

'No, no, it's fine.'

'Okay, well can I do anything else for you, master?' I joke, half expecting a whole list of demands but I feel so bad about his book that I'd happily do them all now.

'No, no. I think we'll call this deal thing quits now, there's only a few more hours left and you've kept your side of the bargain,' he says flatly, not looking at me.

'Really? I don't mi…'

'Yep, I'm tired too so gonna get an early night,' he cuts across me, his face and tone the most serious I've ever known. 'Thanks for the err bath.'

'Right, okay then, night.'

'Night.' He leaves the bathroom quickly and closes the door behind him. I pick up the book and flick through it to examine any damage done. He's right, it will be fine, there are a few big splashes of water, it will probably wrinkle the pages a little but that it's. Like he said, it could be a lot worse, it could have caught on fire from the candles or be completely drenched and the words blurred forever.

Why is he acting so off with me?

Willow's tending to her mum at the hospice so I'm at work alone, holding the fort. I decided to get in early again, apparently a new habit of mine and avoid the morning antics with Liam that admittedly I've grown to like a little too much over the last few weeks. Today however would have just been awkward. Last night when I went to bed, I racked my brains as to why he suddenly turned cold. Maybe he felt odd at the whole bath thing and I crossed a line when I splashed him and accidently touched something else. My cheeks turn red at the thought of it and I hide behind the aloe vera plant on the desk, despite no one being here, except for me. Paranoia sweeps over me. What if he's seeing someone? But it was him that suggested the stupid bath. He really needs to get over himself if that is the case. An image of him silently reciting the poem plays over in my mind. It was a rather odd thing to get me to read.

I stare down at a blank piece of paper and decide to focus my attention elsewhere. The shop. It doesn't open for another hour so if I get my head down, I can write down all the ideas that have been swimming around in my head since the news got out about Mr Woodling becoming a threat to us and potentially trying to take over the shop. My idea is that even if Willow is forced out of her premises, she can still continue her business online. Worst case scenario of course as we aren't going to leave without a fight.

Business plan for Aloe Lovely

1. *Seek out local cafés, hotels/B&Bs and see if they need any plants – offer a maintenance plan as well so can generate income from that too.*
2. *Increase online presence – get Willow online talking about her plants – show her how to create videos for social media etc.*
3. *Update the website*
4. *Network with affluent locals and see if they require plants. A house a month would benefit the business massively.*

My phone beeps on the table and the name Kathy flashes up. I immediately panic that something bad has happened. Kathy rarely texts me.

Kathy: *Hi, I don't mind you using my things but could you just ask first. Also, you used my special bath bomb that Harry got me so I'll be needing that replaced asap. x*

Me: *Hi Kathy, oh my God I'm so sorry. Of course, I'll replace everything.*

Kathy: *Thanks.*

I send the text and groan as I search the fridge for pickled gherkins. That was Kathy's stuff but why did it have LM written on it? I groan again because now Kathy thinks I rifle through her things when in fact I thought it was Liam Murphy's wash bag but I can hardly tell her that or that will lead to a whole load of questions, like why was I in the bathroom with Liam. Now it makes sense, the glittery bath bomb and the lavender bath wash. Of course, it all belonged to Kathy. I make a mental note to pop to the shops before I head home, I'll have to replace her stuff and buy her a bar of grovelling chocolate and a bottle of wine to say sorry. I'm so embarrassed. I spend the rest of my time dusting the shelves and watering and rearranging the plants before the mornings first customers grace us with their presence. A couple of women pop into the shop, I smile and say hello but when I offer to help, they say they're just browsing. I can't help but listen in on their conversation as I busy myself with more plant watering.

'Did you hear about the tarot lady down the road?' one says to the other.

'No, but I've heard she's amazing.'

'Not just good, she's definitely legit, told me that Adam would propose and even told me that it would be a sapphire stone.'

The other lady gasps and the newly engaged nods along. 'Yep, I don't know a single person that's been in there that hasn't come out gob smacked.'

I scoff and the two women turn to look at me.

'Sorry, just had something in my throat, probably just a few cacti spikes.' I feign another cough then give them the thumbs up to let them know that I'm okay. They smile politely and continue their chat about the tarot lady and how amazing she is whilst I silently disagree in the corner. If that's what people are saying then I must be the only one that got a dud reading because mine was utter rubbish. *The reunion is coming and the escort will bear a scar on his jaw. Pay attention to the escort.* Yeah right, he was bloody Del Boy or one of the guys from *lock stock and two smoking barrels* as Willow described him. *The laughs will be plenty and new love is challenging but just around the corner for you.* She couldn't have been more wrong. Oh well, I probably needed that to get over my obsession with wanting to know my future and spending all my money on tarot readings. It's not necessarily a bad thing that she got it wrong.

The rest of the day is very busy which is nice, I'm looking forward to telling Willow what the takings are; she will be pleased. I go outside to bring in the sign and the outdoor plants, reminding myself that I must go to the shop before I go home and replace Kathy's smellies. I'm just collapsing down the sign when someone taps me on the shoulder.

'Mr Woodling,' I say with eyes wide. He smiles warmly at me.

'So sorry to have startled you and just call me Lawrence, please.'

'Are you alright? My sister not giving you any more grief?' He beams.

'Your sister?' I screw my face up then quickly rearrange it back to professional mode.

'Well, Missy's my step-sister. She's fine really, just a bit bossy but I guess that comes with being very ambitious, that's one thing we have in common.'

'I've not seen her since she's done the pop-up shop, she had some lovely things in her store,' I say, evenly. He nods and smiles again. 'She's quite the entrepreneur isn't she?' I continue.

'She is, she has many a side hustle that one, don't tell her I told you but those boat shoes she sells,' he says, with a twinkle in his eye. 'They belong to all of her ex-boyfriends.' I snort at Lawrence's comment, not entirely sure whether he's joking or not.

'My friend tells me the philodendron is still keeping well, a beautiful plant for clearing the air I hear,' he says.

'Yes, it is,' I say slowly, eyeing him suspiciously. What does he want? He's very attractive. It takes me a second to realise that it should be me asking all the questions and finding out the lay of the land and not him.

'Well, I must be off, see you around.'

'Umm, wait,' I shout and Mr Woodling turns around. 'Yes?'

'Can I, I mean, can we go for a drink sometime, I'd like to, I mean, it would be good to discuss more plants with you.' Oh God this isn't going well. His face lights up nevertheless. 'Because there are so many other plants good for air and energy, you'll be quite surprised.' I nod enthusiastically.

'Oh, would it?' Mr Woodling glides back over and we exchange numbers and before I know it, I'm meeting him tomorrow night.

Fucculent my life.

Chapter 20

Mr Woodling, or should I say Lawrence, messaged as soon as I got on the bus last night and by the time I'd got home the meeting was arranged for the following evening. Now here I am, at the bar of one of the swankiest hotels in Coolsbay. The veranda has so many outdoor heated lamps that it's actually warmer to sit outside than it is inside and that's saying something in the middle of a bitterly cold February. I order myself a double vodka and coke and step outside towards the warm glowing lights, pulling my rising hat down over my ears. I'm tempted to drink tonight, I have to find out what his plans are.

Mr Woodling is already sitting outside on a cream sofa waiting for me. He's wearing his casual clothes which consist of the patchwork trousers, a dark blue hoodie and fingerless gloves. His hair has been gelled into a Mohawk again. Apart from the first time he came into the shop, he looks very different from the guy in the suit that occasionally walks by Aloe Lovely. I watch him sip his coffee as he keeps his eyes on the sea view of Coolsbay. I wonder what he's thinking, what evil plan he's hatching? I've decided he must be evil if he's related to that witch Missy Temple, although he doesn't seem it, this could be all a show. A wolf in sheep's clothing.

'Hey, lovely out here, isn't it?' I say evenly, as I arrive at the table.

Mr Woodling jumps up and immediately pulls me into a warm embrace before lightly kissing me on the cheek. He smells delicious despite him being a small business destroyer. 'It is lovely, as are you,' he says.

I wish he wasn't so attractive; it would be much easier if he wasn't so pleasant looking with impeccable manners. To my surprise an image of Liam at the reunion flashes in my mind's eye then an image of him in the bath closely follows. A rush of sadness overcomes me, we haven't spoken since then and I've only briefly seen him once and that was just before I came out this evening. He's upset with me for ruining his book.

'Thank you,' I mumble then sit down.

'So, what made you want to...' Lawrence points his fingers between him and I as he gives me a wry smile. I look down at my feet. Let's nip this in the bud now before Lawrence gets any ideas. As lovely as he is, the shop is my priority right now. 'I got you a drink by the way, vodka and coke, is that alright?'

'Fine, thank you,' I say, taking a sip and then trying not to wince. After such a long break from the alcohol, it now tastes like paint striper. 'I need to be straight with you and talk business. Is that alright?' I say, perched on the edge of my seat with a poker straight back. My hair cascades down my shoulders and I fight the urge to flick it.

'Business?' Lawrence arches his brow then takes a sip of his drink.

'Yep. I'm just going to come out with it.'

'Okay, go for it.' He gesticulates towards me. 'I'm all ears.'

I inhale a deep shaking breath then start my plea. 'Please don't steal Willow's shop, she's worked so very hard to get it to where it needs to be and we have big plans for the business. It's not just her livelihood, it's her life. She needs this more than ever. Her mum is ill you see, well on death's door in fact so if you took this away then I'm not sure she'd be able to cope. She needs it and actually so do I, very much so. It's kept me sane.' There, I've said it. But what surprises me the most is the fact that I've said I need the shop too, because I do. It's saved me in more ways than one. 'Plus, the customers are very fond of us, very loyal in fact. We are THE plant shop of Coolsbay so you'd be silly to compete with us, really. There's nowhere else that cares for plants like we do.' I shrug as Lawrence's mouth falls open. I just hope I've appealed to his human side and he isn't an uncaring psychopath. He sits back and composes himself before speaking slowly.

'You lured me here to tell me that?' He raises both eyebrows and I open my mouth to reply when he lets out an almighty raucous laugh, slapping thighs and everything. A few of the other tables look over at us but Lawrence is not phased.

'What's so funny?' I gulp. He finds my plea hilarious but he's going to do it anyway? He *is* a psychopath.

'Where have you got this from?' He shakes his head, appearing incredulous.

'I have my sources,' I say, sounding exactly like my source, Malcolm. Except Malcolm's sounding like the least reliable source right now.

'Well, if I was looking for a premises it certainly wouldn't be Aloe Lovely. No offence.'

'No?'

'No.'

'Then why am I hearing that you want to buy us out? Offer Willow's landlord more money.' I grimace.

'I want to do nothing of the sort, it's way too small.' He frowns.

'I'm sorry? So just to be clear you don't want to pay the landlord more money and essentially buy us out of Aloe Lovely?'

'I absolutely do not want to do that. We have a premises, it's a little run down but my business partner got us a very good deal. He used to work there by all accounts. That's the bonus of being a local, I'm a London type as you Coolsbayaians say.' He chuckles to himself and I smile nervously.

'Right.' I lean back in my chair then down the rest of my vodka and coke, without trying to heave. Half relieved he doesn't want to steal our premises but now worried he's going to be competing on a much larger scale. He is a London type after all, they come down here and snap up all the best homes and premises. Lawrence's face erupts into a lop-sided smile as he looks at me quizzically.

'Another one?' he asks, as I watch him try to make eye contact with the waiter.

'Yes, okay, but just coke please.' I need to get to the bottom of this.

'Of course.' Lawrence calls the waiter over and orders us two more drinks and a tray of nibbles.

'I'm trying to think how these Chinese whispers got so out of hand,' Lawrence says, stroking his jaw.

'Beats me, you know what it's like, everyone knows everyone's business in Coolsbay.'

'Well, evidently not quite.' He laughs. 'But there is a small fragment of truth in it though.'

'Oh, there is?' I ask, then hold my breath.

'Yes, I've been in talks with a friend to open up a hatha yoga studio.'

'So not another plant shop?'

'No, not another plant shop.' He shakes his head quickly, clearly sick of my seemingly neurotic ways. My body exhales air like a giant whoopie cushion making a weird creaking noise that thankfully Lawrence doesn't notice. 'We had been looking for premises,' he continues. 'And in fact I wanted to ask you ladies to supply me with some plants. Greg and I have always admired the plants and just the general loveliness of you ladies. It's so in keeping with what we want to do.'

'You have? You do?'

'For sure, I think you already know my business partner, Greg anyway.'

'Do I? How would I know him?'

'He lives above the shop.' The waiter serves us our drinks and a tray of olives, nuts and cheese. I take a cube of cheese.

'The Shmoo?' my mouth blurts out through a mouthful of cheese before I have the chance to stop it.

'The who?'

'Sorry, that's what I meant to say, who, I mean who is that?'

Mr Woodling frowns and smiles at the same time, probably now thinking that I'm completely bonkers. 'Greg, my business partner.' He studies my face.

'No, I mean I think I know who he is, but he's never been in the shop to my knowledge.'

'Oh really? He's probably saving himself, wants to do the introductions properly.'

For a whole year? I think, but I don't say it. 'Okay.' Now it's my time to smile and frown at the same time. God this is painful.

'Yes,' Lawrence continues. 'With the owner, Willow, did you say her name was?'

'Yes, that's right. Would you like me to talk to her? I'm taking care of all things business at the moment, given my boss's personal circumstances.'

'Of course. We'd just like to set up a meeting with her and have a chat about what plants we could incorporate into our studio. Perhaps one of those gardens on the wall things would be good.'

'No problem at all, I think I have a good idea what she'll say but I'll double check and come back to you and I'm sure she'd want to sit down with you in person anyway.' She's going to fucking lose her shit. The Shmoo wants a meeting with her. Finally she'll get to talk to him. I'm so excited for her I could scream, but what's taken him so bloody long! Why hasn't he been in to say hello? It's so strange!

'Fantastic,' Mr Woodling says, looking almost as relieved as I feel.

'Oh, and Mr Woodling.'

'Lawrence, please.'

'We'd be happy to supply you with plants for your new studio, would you know of anywhere else that might require our services? Hotels? Restaurants? Businesses? The Garden walls, I mean the living walls would work fantastically in any of these places,' I say, surprising myself at my own entrepreneurial skills.

'I'll ask about,' he says, as his eyes move off into the distance and one of his arms shoots up. 'Jean-Paul,' he calls to a man in a white shirt and slicked back hair. 'This wonderful lady works at Aloe Lovely and they're branching out to supply plants to businesses. Could your place do with a bit of plant action?'

'Plant action?' he questions in a thick French accent.

'Hmmm Possible, do you have a business card or a brochure I could browse?' I wince at my unprofessionalism; I don't think Willow even has business cards.

'Not on me I'm afraid but if you give me your business card then I could email you with some information and a link to our website?'

'Oui, perfect, nice to meet you, uumm...'

'Lottie, nice to meet you too, Jean-Paul.'

'I must go, I have a huge party arriving in ten minutes and I need to kick some staffs' butts,' he says, before checking his watch.

'No problem, Jean-Paul, take care.'

We both watch him sashay off into the hotel and I try my best to hold in excited squeals.

'Thank you, Lawrence.' I grin. Excited for the future of Aloe Lovely.

'No problem, so do you have a boyfriend?'

'Hey Lottie, where have you been? Well, don't you look just lovely.' Kathy beams as she looks up from her cross-stitch which is something resembling a valentine's message, adorned with hearts and flowers. It's pretty impressive and I imagine it hanging above their bed like an old married couple, an old married couple who do loud sex screams. I shudder and shake my head to rid it of the audible memory. Thank God she's forgiven me for using her bath stuff, or rather for Liam using her bath stuff.

Harry sits beside her and Liam sits in the arm chair in the corner of the living room. Harry gives me a little wave and Liam looks up briefly, offers a half smile then looks back down again at his phone. He can't still be pissed off at me about getting his book wet, surely? It wasn't even that damaged. Just a bit of wrinkled paper from the water splashes.

I'm sick of this shit.

'Oh, hot business date.' I wink at Kathy as she arranges her mouth into an ooo shape and sets her cross-stitch to one side.

'With whom?' she asks.

'Mr Woodling, he's very keen.' I pause, feeling a little ballsy after my one vodka and coke. 'About my business ideas.' After Lawrence's rather forward question, I actually said I was unavailable as far as relationships go but Liam doesn't need to know that and in fact, I'm enjoying the look on his face too much to say it was strictly business. Call me a petty bitch if you like. Lawrence is good looking but I'd never mix business with pleasure, especially as it isn't actually *my* business to mess with. He didn't seem too bothered by my refusal and I'm sure he isn't short of offers anyway. I may have mentioned to Lawrence that I heard that the tarot lady was single and she's very pretty and sweet, despite giving me a dud reading. I guess all psychics have their off days but I won't be going back to find out. Those days are gone. I think of NextlevelNyssa and her mindfulness posts. That's what I aspire to be, living in the present, not obsessing over the future or the past.

'You should get in there, sis. I've heard he's loaded.' Harry adds. 'Has his fingers in many pies, a real business mind.'

'Maybe I have,' I lie and look at Liam, not being able to help myself. He's cross at me for no reason and I'm enjoying winding him up. 'Yes, I've heard, like his sister so I hear.' I'm still shocked that they are related.

'Who's his sister?' Kathy asks.

'That Missy Temple, right bitch. Not like Lawrence at all, he's SO lovely,' I say, over egging my admiration for him. Harry glances at Liam who looks back at him with a look as if to say, Don't. You. Dare. The look is lost on my brother, of course.

'Hey, Missy? Isn't that the girl you're seeing, Liam?' Harry says, in a cheerful tone, excited to present Liam and I with some common ground. 'Mate, isn't that the girl you're seeing?' he repeats.

'No, I just work for her,' Liam replies, not looking up from his phone.

'Ooooh, easy now tiger.' Harry laughs and Liam looks up to grin back at him.

'Missy?' Her name forces its way out of my mouth a little too abruptly and I tell myself to reel it in. You don't care. You don't care about Liam. He was just a fake boyfriend. No loyalties. He can date or seemingly shag whoever he likes. 'Since when?' I hear myself ask as my heart drops into my stomach. He doesn't reply. 'I didn't know you worked for her, thought you just did this and that. . .' my voice trails off. I'd assumed he did odd jobs for people like painting and putting up shelves if needed. I didn't think he worked for an actual person, not least Missy the witch.

'Oh wow, you guys! We could all go on a triple date!' Kathy claps her hands together with glee. 'One big happy family,' she continues. 'And it really would be because, Liam is like another sibling, he bickers with you, Lottie, more than you and Harry do.'

'Yep, one big happy family,' I say slowly. 'Isn't that sweet?' I continue. I try to keep my tone even and steady. I fail and the word sweet sounds as if I have a smoking habit of forty cigarettes a day. Liam looks up from his phone, a flash of concern across his face. He treats me to a big beautiful smile and his twinkling blue eyes hold my gaze for longer than necessary. Has he forgiven me now?

Chapter 21

The doorbell rings.

'I'll get it,' I say flatly, as Liam begins to get up, flashing me another big smile which now resembles something between pity and embarrassment. His blue eyes, not twinkling anymore, study me with curiosity.

'No, it's fine, it's for me anyway,' he says, but I'm almost at the door now, the handle already in my hand.

'Hi,' I say, probably looking like a startled rabbit caught in headlights. I've only just found out about this and suddenly here she is on my doorstep. The cheek.

'Oh hey.' Missy blinks back at me. 'It's you.' She stands very still, except for one little finger twitching by her side. The witch bitch itch is clearly too much for her.

'Yes it's me,' I reply.

Missy snaps out of her trance, a smirk slowly spreading across her face. 'Are you the live-in maid that Liam talks about?' She chortles to herself as I look at her unsmilingly.

'Excuse me?'

'Oh, it's just that Liam said that...'

'Hey, Missy, shall we go now?' Liam's voice booms from behind me, the Irish lilt sending my neck into a flurry of goosebumps despite my growing feelings of contempt for him. I glance at Missy who smooths down her blonde bob and purses her lips. She's noticed.

'Hey you,' she purrs at Liam, pawing at his chest to bring him closer to her. 'Yes, yes let's go,' she continues.

'Have a great time,' I sing into Liam's ear a little too enthusiastically.

He brushes past me to get to her, Missy the mega bitch, I'm shocked, appalled and disgusted. Well, as far as I'm concerned they're welcome to each other. I wonder how Missy would feel if I told her that I'd been reading to her boyfriend in the bath the other night, all part of my maid's service of course. I smirk at the memory. 'Doing anything nice?' I ask, not being able to help myself.

'We're going to the new Thai restaurant on the harbour, Liam's been helping me decorate it, haven't you cupcake?' she gushes. Cupcake? Yuck. Liam grimaces then forces his face into a smile. She seems keen on him. His shoes are safe for now.

'Yes, Missy and I worked together on the project so tonight we're celebrating its completion, complimentary meal and drinks on them.' He doesn't sound excited. He *should* sound excited.

'That's right, we worked very hard, didn't we? With my interior design skills and your decorating skills, we make the perfect team.' She leans forward and kisses him on the cheek and a fresh rage boils within me.

'Yes, I can see that.' Both fake. Both up their own arses. 'Well, enjoy your evening.' I close the door abruptly on their faintly bemused faces then turn around and lean against the door, eyes closed, inhaling a big shaking breath. Perhaps I will take Mr Woodling up on his offer of a date, he's nice looking, business focused and kind, he really isn't a bad catch at all. But he isn't

Liam and despite myself I'm longing for the road trip Liam, the reunion Liam, the thoughtful housemate Liam, the lovely Liam. But it looks like somebody else has beaten me to it because he's a bloody catch too. I just didn't see it until I couldn't have it.

I slope back into the living room to see my phone flashing with a text. As if this day couldn't get any worse.

Willow: *The inevitable has happened, mum passed away peacefully in her sleep yesterday afternoon. She had her loved ones around her so wasn't alone. We're making arrangements now and I'll be back in the shop to try and get back to some sort of normality after the funeral.*

Willow: *Is everything holding up okay there? Would it be okay to dump the shop on you again? I'm so sorry. xx*

I slump down on the sofa, hovering my fingers over the keyboard on my phone, not knowing the right thing to say. Harry and Kathy bicker in the kitchen about what to have for dinner as I tentatively type my reply. By the sounds of their bickering, it's going to be a frozen pizza and garlic bread kind of night.

Me: *I'm so so sorry Willow. Of course, leave the shop with me and if there's anything else I can do, please let me know, it's honestly no problem, I can hold the fort, I don't mind at all. xx*

Willow: *Thank you, I appreciate you so much, I really don't know what I would have done without you. I'll definitely pop back as soon as I can, I need some positive plant energy, some big love energy and I miss my shop and having a laugh with you! Any news in the shop? Please keep me updated.*

Me: *We've missed you too, whatever you think is best. I've got it all covered here. Well, Lawrence and Greg want to set up a meeting with you. Possible exciting business ventures on their way.*

Willow: *Who the hell are Lawrence and Greg?*

Me: *Sorry, I mean Mr Woodling and The Shmoo.*

Willow: *What?? The Shmoo has been in the shop and you*

haven't told me!!

Me: *Hehe, I wanted to save it for when I saw you but it's too good not to tell you now. Thought you could do with some good news now.*

Willow: *It is. Please keep me updated on any Shmoo activity. I miss his wavy locks and bouncy walk. Anyway, off to grieve. Speak soon. Xxx*

'It's Pizza tonight,' Harry says, perching on the arm of the other sofa, interrupting my thoughts of Aloe Lovely and Willow. 'You want some?'

'Nah, I'm not really hungry thanks, Hazza. Think I'll go out for a walk in a bit.'

'Okay.' He frowns. 'You alright?' I let out a big sigh and stretch my arms and legs out on the sofa. I wonder what Liam and Missy are talking about? An image of them staring lovingly into each other's eyes creeps into my mind.

'I'll be alright,' I say unconvincingly. I try to shake the thought of Liam and Missy together from my mind meanwhile cringing at my pathetic attempts to make him jealous. I'm better than that now, was it the alcohol? I should have just asked him what was wrong. Maybe I still will. He may be with Missy but we are still friends. She can't ruin that too.

'Want to talk about it?'

'Nope.'

'You sure?'

'Nope on a rope. I don't want to talk.' I close my eyes and feel the ominous burn of tears begin to start. When I open them again, Harry has been replaced with Kathy.

'You sure you're alright?' You've not been yourself,' Kathy says, as she gets up and walks towards me. She plonks herself down next to me on the sofa and rests her hand on my arm.

'Yeah, just men problems, life choice issues, you know, the usual.'

'Oh, I thought you were going to date that Mr Woodling guy? Happy families and all that.' She smiles with just her top teeth showing.

'Yeah, I'm not so sure about that now, plus you shouldn't mix business with pleasure. I wouldn't want to mess things up for Willow. What if we got together and it didn't work out and then he decided to take his business elsewhere?'

'Oh no,' Kathy says slowly and ominously, as she rests a hand on her cheek.

'What?' I sit up straight.

'It's Liam, isn't it? I knew it. The constant bickering followed by the sickening flirting. I said to Harry about it but you know what he's like, about observant as a drunken sloth.' She giggles at her own joke and I put both my hands on my cheeks, feeling them burn with embarrassment.

'Oh Kathy, is it that obvious?'

'Yes, now I really think about it. It is. Oh Yuck.' She jumps off the sofa and looks at me in mock disgust. 'You haven't done it on our sofa have you? Our lovely new sofa,' she whines.

'No, no, we haven't done it on the sofa, we haven't done IT at all, except kiss once at my university reunion.' Butterflies form in my stomach as Kathy raises her eyebrows then picks up a doily on the coffee table, she studies it for a second then mops her brow with it.

'Phew.' She laughs then positions herself next to me again, still holding the doily. 'So tell me all about it.'

So I spend the next twenty minutes telling her all about it, the breakfasts, the reunion, the stolen looks and brief electric touches, even the bath, until Harry walks in with the not so edible looking pizza.

'So it was Liam who used all my stuff?' Kathy says.

'Well no, not Liam, it was me, I thought it was his wash bag because it had LM on it. You know, Liam Murphy.'

'Oh.' Kathy giggles then blushes before putting her hand over her mouth. 'Harry bought me that washbag.'

'What does LM stand for then?'

They both smirk at each other. A private joke.

'Actually, don't tell me. I don't want to know.' I make a face and pretend to gag.

'No, no, it's not that bad. It just stands for Little Minx,' Harry says unconvincingly and Kathy does an out of character purr at him.

'Really?' I say, raising an eyebrow and Kathy giggles again. A secret couples joke. 'I don't know what LM stands for but it definitely isn't Little Minx, but that's bad enough so please don't tell me what it actually stands for.' They both laugh again then focus on eating the pizza as despite telling it not to, my overactive brain desperately tries to work out what it stands for. Lady Muck, Lovely Melons, Loud masturbater. It's got to be the latter if listening to their sex screams is anything to go by.

'Careful, don't get crumbs on my bed,' I grin.

'So,' Harry says in-between mouthfuls of pizza. 'My mate Beau and his party bike has been confirmed for the first of March, he's giving tours of Coolsbay again, it's going to be a good laugh.'

'But I'm not going on it, I don't want a peanut to the eye and almost go blind again,' Kathy says all matter-of-fact as she blinks rapidly.

'What's happening on the first of March?' I ask.

'What? The annual Coolsbay party of course.'

'Hmm, but will it rain? Kathy pipes up.

'Oh, I completely forgot about that, it's definitely going to rain,' I say without hesitation.

'Oh you're such a grump, Lottie. What would Liam call you if he were here? Grumpy Grotty.' He chortles and Kathy gives him a dig in the ribs.

'I don't think it will rain,' Kathy says, smiling kindly at me. 'I think the sun will shine bright.'

'Ever the optimist, Kathy,' Harry says, kissing her on the lips. 'I hope you're right.'

Harry ends up suggesting wine to cheer me up, so we all have a few glasses followed by more snacks until I can't keep my eyes open any longer and I boot Harry and Kathy out of their own living room so I can finally go to sleep. It's been a weird old day of change and uncertainty and I'm not sure what to think of a lot of things, Liam and Missy being the main confusion. The best and most sensible thing to do would be to go straight to sleep; everything's better after a good night's sleep but I can't, the alcohol is keeping me awake and it's actually made me feel really ill. As I lie in bed feeling rough, I visit my favourite corner of the internet to cheer myself up, NextLevelNyssa.

I'm surprised to see a perfectly poised Nyssa, sitting on the floor of a very boring looking multi story car park, much like the one we have here at Coolsbay shopping centre. She's on a stripy rainbow coloured rug, with her back facing us as usual. This time her shiny dark bob hangs down covering her neck tattoo. Her legs are crossed and her perfectly manicured fingers are placed on her knees facing up to the ceiling of the grey stone building. A couple of pigeons are perched on the ledge of the car park and I imagine them dropping big bird shits on to her face. I wonder if she'd still be so poised or simply congratulate them for not being constipated and being able to relieve themselves so freely? I also wonder again why she chooses to hide her face before reading her carefully crafted caption.

Choosing to be happy wherever you are takes that inner strength that will keep you grounded. Whether you're in a dull car park or a stunning luxurious beach resort, take the time to count your blessings. Remember, it's not where you are that matters but who you're with and how you choose to position your mindset. You have a choice. Choose happiness or choose to be the martyr.

The choice is entirely yours.

Chapter 22

The next few weeks go by in a work crazy, plant indulgent haze.

If my fingers weren't green before from all the gherkins I eat then they certainly are now from all the plants that I've been touching. I throw myself into getting Aloe Lovely looking perfect for Willow's return, as well as marketing the brand on social media. Ferns, philodendron and other foliage fills the shop and I stand back to admire the huge bird of paradise plant that I've just finished cleaning. In the meantime, I also receive an email from Jean-Paul asking when I can meet with him to discuss plants to enhance the classy, comforting ambience in the hotel.

An image of Brandon's obnoxious face peering through the cheese plants at the university reunion pops into my mind's eye. Definitely some cheese plants. I take a moment to silently thank him for acting like a complete dick and almost ruining my life. If it wasn't for him leaving me out on my arse then I wouldn't have discovered my talent for social media marketing and an enjoyment for green fingered goodness.

Instantaneously a whoosh of sadness overcomes me, when Willow is back, I'll be back to part-time hours and part-time pay and we all know that isn't a viable or sustainable option by any means. If I want to become a real, proper grown up with my finances under control then I need a full-time income in order to achieve it. I never did hear from those jobs I applied for. Despite still living with him, I haven't seen much of Liam. At the moment we're like passing ships in the night. He tried to talk to me about the bath incident the night after but it all seemed to go downhill from there. Just the two of us were in the kitchen one evening as I was getting a glass of water before bed. He padded over to me and leant on the shiny kitchen worktop then uttered the words. 'So, care to talk about the book disaster?' He let out a little nervous laugh, his cheeks pinkened and all I could think about was him and Missy the mega bitch. The look on my face must have not looked too impressed but I was willing to chat as he's my friend and I miss him. The moment I opened my mouth to speak, Harry and Kathy bustled into the kitchen kissing passionately, blissfully unaware that we were there and probably just a few minutes away from the sex screams starting. Liam and I both made our excuses and left. Apart from that fleeting and awkward exchange we've not spoken.

Missy hasn't graced us with her presence again but Liam's been out a lot so no doubt he's living the high life with her in her perfectly decorated and styled house. Such a weird match, I wouldn't have put them together, he's like a ray of sunshine, all bright, bouncy and cheerful and she's like a short sharp ice-cold rain shower. They do say opposites attract. I consider for a moment what weather metaphor that would make me and I decide that at the moment I'd be big black dark looming clouds but I guess normally I'm a mild spring day, on a good day, that is.

I hear Liam's now working on doing up Lawrence's Hatha Yoga studio so it seems it pays to have Missy as a girlfriend. Lawrence wanted to get me in to discuss plants but I've managed to sweet talk him and he's agreed to wait for Willow, the real plant expert. My thinking being that I could avoid bumping into Liam in another awkward setting and Willow can finally meet with Greg the elusive Shmoo. My own love life may be absolutely non-existent but at least my matchmaking plan is finally coming together.

'Care for a treat?' Malcolm shuffles into the shop holding a paper bag in each hand. My stomach begins to grumble aggressively.

'Malc,' I say evenly. 'How are you?'

'Good, good can't complain,' he says, as he slowly edges towards me, a look of worry etched on his face.

'Is Willow back yet? I've made her something special.' He shakes the brown paper bags in his hand along with giving me a sheepish grin. He knows. He knows he's fucked up.

'Yes, she's just popped out to the shop, did you want to wait for her?' I say kindly because I could go to town on him about all the gossiping and shit stirring he's caused but we all know Malc's a gossip. Instead of fretting about him and over analysing everything he was saying I should have gone straight to the horse's mouth itself in the first place.

Malc's gossiping, as strange as it sounds, almost always comes from a place of love, even if he doesn't realise it himself. He just wants to keep people informed or form a connection with people because he's lonely. He told Willow once that being on his own for twenty years has taken its toll and he often talks to inanimate objects in his house as if they're people. We're all fighting our own demons so a little bit of empathy goes a long way when someone isn't acting in the perfect way. But I'll be closing myself off from any gossip now, shutting it down, we can talk about other things such as current affairs or plans for the future. God I sound like Kathy. People like Malc are normally just broken beings in some form, too bitter or bored with their own lives.

'Oooh, yes okay, I will wait. Hey I've got something to tell you I...'

'Now now,' I say firmly but kindly and very much reminding myself of Mary Poppins. Malcolm gives me a puzzled stare. 'So, how are you, Malcolm? How's business?' I continue, flashing him a warm smile. He looks bemused for a second before shuffling uncomfortably from side to side. A small smile plays across his lips. 'Actually, I'm okay, I've recently met someone,' he almost squeaks and my heart leaps for him.

'Aww that's lovely Malc, what's she like?' I ask and his face lights up.

'She's pretty and loves my cakes and she makes the most delicious cottage pie. Bit of a green fingered expert as well.' He nods towards me. 'It's early days but I'm hopeful this is the start of something special.'

'Well, I'm so happy for you.' I grin. This is depressing. Even Malcolm's love life is better than mine. Liam's face flashes in my mind, his bright blue eyes sparkling with joy. God, I so miss being around him. This avoiding each other thing is excruciating. Something's got to give soon.

'Business is slow,' Malc continues, as he begins to wring his hands. 'It's not like it used to be thirty years ago. Everything is online now and those fancy cake shops with the free selfie sticks steal all the biz.' I haven't heard the word selfie stick in about five years; he may be more behind the times than he thinks. A little lightbulb pings in my brain.

'It is. Times have changed a lot. I've helped Willow with her online presence and marketing and it's really made a difference. I could help you too, if that's something you'd like to explore?' Wait, am I masquerading as a social media marketing expert? No. I am one and especially to Malcolm.

'Well yes, that might not be a bad idea, that video you did for me did attract more attention to the shop. I would pay you of course, I'm desperate to sell more buns and pastries and I don't know why I'm not. Everyone always tells me how tasty they are.'

'They are Malc, you just need to market yourself correctly but I can help you with that, we'll get the whole of Coolsbay wanting a feel of your buns in no time.'

Malcolm chortles at my pun and I laugh along with him.

'Oi, don't steal my only employee, I need her you know,' Willow teases, as she appears next to Malc. Willow's got so thin after losing her mum, a few of Malcolm's pastries are just what she needs.

'Oh, I was just. It was just…' I stutter. Shit. Touting for business in my friend's shop whilst I'm working here is probably not the best idea.

'It's fine,' she says softly. 'I can't keep you forever and you need to branch out and earn a full-time wage. I'm well aware of that. In fact, I think it's a wonderful idea.' She winks at Malcolm and takes one of the paper bags from his hands. 'Us small businesses could all do with a little Lottie marketing magic.'

'Really? I grin.

'Really,' Willow says, as she pulls me into a hug before setting her pastry down on the side.

'That's not a bad name for it you know,' I say

thoughtfully.

'Lottie's Marketing Magic?' Malcolm pipes up. 'It does have a certain ring to it.'

'Yes, it does indeed.' Willow smiles then gives me a knowing nod as she goes to say hello to a regular customer who's just walked in. Malcolm beams at me as I take a bite of his pastry. I make all the hmmmm and so yummy noises as thoughts of my new business venture buzz excitedly around my brain like fireworks. Is this my thing? Is this what I'm going to do now? I don't know but one thing I know is that I feel bloody excited about it.

'How do I look? Do I look too gaunt? Christ I do, I look gaunt, don't I? Like I'm a corpse that's just been dug up.' Willow swoops her long blonde hair to one side and purses her pale pink, painted lips as she peer at herself in her compact mirror. Her mother's death has taken its toll a little but she's still stunning.

'You look beautiful,' I say. 'And you're going to blow them away. Also, I just love the outfit.' Willow twirls around in a tight-fitting long-sleeved dress that has pictures of different cacti all over it, as I spray my hair with a bit of de-frizzing oil. The shop is now closed and instead of us getting ready to go out for drinks, which we used to spend our spare time doing when I first joined the shop, we're getting ready for our first business meeting with Lawrence and Greg aka Mr Woodling and The Shmoo.

'He's just so bloody gorgeous, The Shmoo, ahh I mean Greg,' Willow says, as I giggle. 'I don't even know what he sounds like, oh God, what if he has a really bad speech impediment or sounds like *Micky Mouse*? That will completely ruin my fantasy of him forever. I've built him up to be this god.'

'He's going to sound perfectly normal and just be cool, it will be fine.'

'I know, I need to remember that this is a business meeting and not a date. I'm acting like a D and D,' Willow says.

'What's that?'

'Desperate and Divorced,' she says, as I smirk into my pickled gherkin. 'It's just so odd, we've never actually met but we've made up this whole backstory about him. What if he doesn't live up to the expectations. What if he isn't a good dad or doesn't have a job? What if he is really bloody boring? Oh Fucculent, I'm doing it again!' Wow, Willow has really got it bad, she's normally chill vibes only, I've never seen her this flustered in the whole time I've known her. 'Slap me.' Willow blinks back at me.

'What?'

'Just fucking slap me around the face and knock some sense into me.'

'No!' I laugh.

'Please, I'm going mad. I need a quick, sharp, shock. Just slap me. SLAP ME. SLAP ME,' Willow scream laughs hysterically.

'Umm, okay,' I squeal, as my hand swipes at her face. I miss the first time and we both scream with laughter then I hit her again, the slap making a loud smack as my hand hits her cheek. Shit. That was a hard slap, even my hand hurts.

'OUCH.' Willow's hand flies up to her cheek as she stares at me in shock.

'What in the?' A booming male voice says as Willow and I freeze rooted to the spot.

It's Lawrence and Greg.

Chapter 23

Willow and I stand, rooted to the spot.

Her hand, still on her cheek and our mouths wide open.

'I told her to do it, had a mosquito buzzing around me that just wouldn't go away,' Willow whimpers, still holding her cheek. 'You get loads of bugs in a plant shop, it's all food to them,' she explains, with a forced laugh.

The Shmoo aka Greg steps forward. He swooshes his wavy golden brown hair over to one side and glides over to Willow, his face etched with concern. He winces as he gently takes her hand off her face to reveal a big red hand print. 'Ooooh ouch.' His expression relaxes slightly and he smiles a big toothy grin.

A shy smile spreads across Willow's lips. 'It was a massive mosquito,' Willow tells Greg.

'It was. A massive one. Really big,' I pipe up and nod as I watch the bewildered Willow melt in The Shmoo's presence. He lightly touches her cheek again and looks at her as if she's new-found treasure. Lawrence, who has been watching this exchange with me the whole time, clears his throat loudly and eyeballs Greg.

'Umm, so we thought we'd surprise you ladies and come to you first,' Lawrence says. 'Greg wants to have a look around the shop too, he's more visual than audio and perhaps we can peruse some plants that we like the look of and then you ladies can advise if they'll be suitable.'

Greg flashes Willow another perfect smile. So strange he hasn't visited before. He seems different to the Shmoo that would smile into his own reflection every time he walked past, or was he simply looking for Willow, the smiles meant for her?

'Umm, we brought coffee.' Lawrence nods towards the cardboard carrier in his hand which holds four takeaway coffees.

'Ooh thank you,' Willow says as Greg takes the carrier and offers coffees out to Willow and I. We all faff around for a bit in an awkward silence, pouring and stirring in sugar and sipping on boiling hot coffee.

'So would you like the grand tour of all the plants?' I ask cheerily, with a mouth warmer than the sun.

'Oh yes, please,' Lawrence replies.

Greg nods again with a silly grin on his face. He's awfully quiet, not what I expected at all. He must be extremely shy. Willow takes us on a tour of all the plants in her shop showing off the new string of pearls (that literally look like a string of pearls) and moss balls that have just been delivered. While Lawrence asks questions, The Shmoo remains perfectly silent. He seems to be taking it all in, nodding in all the right places and making all the right noises at the plants but he hasn't said a word so far and he hasn't taken his eyes off Willow. He's been completely mute.

'So, the Shhm, I mean Greg,' Willow says pointedly, after she's finished giving a detailed talk about how palms are amazing for big open spaces and that they don't take much care. 'Do you have any thoughts on what plants you'd like for the studio?'

Greg blinks back at her, again saying nothing.

'Any thoughts on the plants?' she tries again, as Greg goes completely beetroot, matching the colour of one of Missy Temples fancy scarves. Lucky he didn't get that one or it would clash horribly with his skin. Missy Temple, even her name screams bitch. Who names their kid Missy if they don't want them to be a complete brat? And she certainly lives up to it. I look at Lawrence, such a kind, helpful man. I still can't believe they're related.

'Greg is significantly hard of hearing,' Lawrence says softly, touching his friend on the arm. 'He can lip read great though.'

'Oh, you should have said before. I can sign. My son's deaf,' Willow says excitedly, as she signs the words with her hands. It's been a while since I've seen Willow sign as her son is grown up and has moved away now but it's fascinating and quite impressive to see. Lawrence and I watch on as Greg and Willow become ensconced in a silent communication that only they can understand. Lips move and noises are made as hands flail around in eager communication. The hands speed up until Willow gasps and her hand flies up to her mouth.

Greg wiggles his hips and holds back his hair then they both laugh at something that Willow has signed that leaves Greg doubled over for a moment, he guffaws silently with the occasional loud honk, reminding me of the noise that those confident Canadian geese makes. Greg sweeps back his hair again and I glance at Lawrence as his eyes widen before he smiles and shrugs. He has no idea what they're saying either and for a moment I imagine subtitles above their heads which probably resemble nothing like what they're talking about but it passes the time nonetheless.

Next, the signing takes on a more serious tone. Willow appears bashful as does Greg who slows down the signing and appears to be doing a lot of the talking with his eyes and head. Willow nods quickly then gives him a beautiful smile, which reminds me of the late Princess Diana, that smile could melt a thousand hearts and so could hers. They eventually finish signing, remembering that Lawrence and I are also in the room and this is supposed to be a business meeting.

'So, guys are you going to enlighten us on your rather colourful exchange?' Lawrence grins as he waves his hands about, clearly as amused by their performance as I am.

'Oh no,' Willow says. 'If you don't know sign language then I'm afraid it can't be repeated. It's a secret club,' she annunciates the word club teasing us as Greg and Lawrence burst into fits of laughter.

Greg signs zipping his lips up before giving Willow a sly and sexy wink. I wouldn't be surprised if he's asked her out for a drink but there was a lot more to that conversation than they're letting on. A part of me wants this meeting to hurry up so I can get Willow alone to ask her.

'Okaaaay, well in that case perhaps we should take you ladies to see the new yoga studio.'

'Oh yes, that would be fantastic,' Willow says, as she signs along.

'Yes fantastic, I'm so excited to see it, I almost wet my plants,' I squawk, as I motion wetting myself with huge sweeping hands down to the floor. Oh no. I'm getting caught up in the hysteria and I'd actually be quite proud of that witty pun except I think I've read that on a gardening sign or a birthday card and fairly recently so it's not even an original. I hold my hands together refraining from doing any more embarrassing hand actions. After all, it's not me who knows sign language. Luckily everyone laughs at my attempt at a joke, whether it's with me or at me, I don't mind, I'm just grateful it wasn't met with an awkward silence.

'Oh Lottie, you're my little ray of sunshine,' Willow sings, as she does the sign for sunshine. I've never been described as that before but I actually quite like it. My mind begins to wander to Liam, he's the real ray of sunshine, even his hair resembles the sun's flames. Perhaps some of his cheery disposition has rubbed off on me. Perhaps I've been a bit harsh and I should make the effort to talk to him, at least hear what he has to say.

Willow locks up and we wander down to the end of the high street until we come to a rather dodgy looking alleyway that I have to say I've never been down before. We walk in single file down the narrow path, hunching our shoulders so as not to brush them against the walls and snag our clothes. We eventually arrive at a rather industrial looking building with high tall windows. The windows have been blacked out and it almost resembles a prison. Someone's graffitied FREE BLOW JOBS HERE followed by an arrow in pink paint just to the left of the vault-like looking door. Willow smirks at me as we wait for Greg to unlock the door with a chunky silver key.

Oh my God, I'm sure this was the old sex club. I thought it was a myth until I met Willow and she regaled me with tales of the times her husband encouraged her go here just so he could hook up with an elusive unicorn (a lone woman looking for sex with a couple) which of course never happened because they're elusive. At that point their relationship was over so she was essentially doing nothing more than facilitating his next fling. She said it was a sad last attempt at saving their failing marriage which had completely lost all of its spice and allure but all it did was open his eyes to all the other women out there and that was the end of that when he met a lady by the name of Gloria. Willow wasn't that fussed though, glad if anything for taking him off her hands. But why are we *here*?

Suddenly NextLevelNyssa's last post pops into my mind. It looked like she was in an industrial building not dissimilar to this one. *It doesn't matter where you are, it's the people you're with and the mindset you're in.*

We follow Greg into the building and up the dark, narrow staircase. At the top of the stairs everything is painted black with a sporadic red love heart dotted about and there's a small office with a window and a till immediately situated to the left of the top step. I imagine the punters paying for their wild night out here along with a packet of condoms and a bottle of lube. I bite my lip so I don't giggle like a silly little school girl.

'Of course, this will all be redecorated,' Lawrence says, as if reading our thoughts. 'So it's in keeping with the zen theme so just ignore all of this for now.' He waves a hand, almost in disgust, at the seedy décor. 'We've got the main room completed anyway, come this way.' We follow him up a couple of stairs and then turn left until we are met with another corridor. Silently we walk in single file along the dark painted corridor. I notice a couple of perfectly round holes cut out in the walls just big enough to fit a golf ball. Peep holes or worse? I resist the urge to stop and have a look. As tempting as it is, I don't think it would be appreciated. We arrive at two double doors, freshly painted white. Greg takes out another key and I hold my breath as we enter the room. His arm reaches up to flick on the switch as we slowly shuffle into the room. I'm still holding my breath as Willow is the first in and the first to gasp. What has she seen? Have they lured us here to tell us that it is in fact naked sex yoga and now we have to do a demo.

Oh God, please no.

There aren't even any plants yet to cover our modesty.

'Oh wow,' she says breathlessly. 'It's just just...' She turns to Greg who signs a word for something and she nods in agreement as their twinkling eyes meet.

'Beautiful.' Lawrence nods. 'I know, my sister and her partner have worked extremely hard. I'm so pleased with it; it even has a unit here with bottle holders and a slot to place your yoga mat in.' The word partner stings more than I thought it would. Does he mean Liam? Is Liam now her boyfriend?

'It's gorgeous,' I agree, as I take in the freshly painted cotton coloured room and stripped wooden flooring. A far cry from the seedy reception area and exterior of the building. One of the walls has a hand painted mural of a forest on it and I imagine the yoga instructor standing in front of it on one leg with arms reaching up to the sky, palms pressed together. It makes me feel free, relaxed and I want to dive in. 'Very serene, perfect for yoga enthusiasts,' I continue as though I know what I'm talking about although I've never done yoga in my life.

'Thank you, so all we need now is your expertise, what plants do you suggest to enhance the serenity?'

Chapter 24

We discuss succulents and plants of all varieties as Greg and Lawrence nod and agree with enthusiasm whilst I'm silently thinking what the actual fucculent? How the fuck did we end up in the old sex club with The Shmoo and Mr Woodling whilst we decide on what plants will add to the ambience in their freshly decorated yoga studio? Newly decorated as Anthony from *Bridgerton* would put it, by *the bain of my existence and the object of my desires*. Except this time, roles are reversed and I'm the feverishly hopelessly head over heels Anthony, and Liam is the head strong, doesn't act arsed Kate.

Speaking of Kates, *This Woman's Work* by Kate Bush plays quietly in the background of our local pub, the Mermaid's Lair and I groan inwardly. The last time I thought about this song was on the road trip to the reunion in Manchester with Liam when he opened up to me about his mum. A sad sigh escapes me that sounds like air being slowly let out of a balloon as Willow glides back over to our table with two drinks, a champagne for her and an elderflower spritzer for me plus two packets of nuts. We've come straight here after our meeting for a debrief.

'I've treated us to the fancy stuff, to new business,' Willow says, as she chinks my glass with hers.

'To new business,' I echo back, as a smirk spreads across my face. 'You still have the slap mark on your cheek.' I giggle as Willow holds her glass up to her pink cheek, soothing it with the cold champagne flute.

'Oh God.' She giggles back. 'What a pair we are. Saying it was a mosquito was the only thing I could think of.'

'And it's February,' I add. 'I don't think you get many of those around this time of year.'

'No, but I was ready to blag it that the temperature inside the shop attracts them whatever the time of year, except they didn't even challenge it.'

'No, because The Shmoo was too busy making eye fucculents with you.'

'Oh stop!' Willow shrieks then looks around to see who is listening, a couple of regulars propped up at the bar, turn around with pints in hand to see what all the fuss is about and I smile sweetly at them.

'Only if you spill. What was all of this in the shop about?' I fling my arms about in an attempt to mimic their theatrical exchange via sign language. Willow throws her head back and laughs, her neck pinking up at the thought of it.

'Well,' she starts, looking around to check if anyone is listening. She lowers her voice and tone. 'You're not going to believe this but do you remember I told you my ex-husband would sometimes talk me into going to the sex club with him to try and spice up our marriage?' I nod eager to know more. 'Our intention was not to specifically do anything with any other couples but to just look around, be inspired as it were.'

'Kind of like watching real life porn?' I say, wrinkling up my nose, trying to make sense of it. Willow considers this for a moment as she takes a sip of her drink.

'Sort of…yeah. . .'

'Go on…'

'Well, it got to a point where, towards the end of our marriage we'd go every month, for about a year and for the last few months Gary started to make friends and got friendly with one woman in particular, the woman he eventually left me for, Gloria. Anyway, they brought in a couple of cage dancers, a man and a woman. I remember the man always had his hair tied up in a bun on the top of his head and he had an incredible body, the way he moved was just divine, so elegant. He can't hear the music that well but he can feel the vibrations of the music in his body.' Her eyes cloud over for a moment as she pictures the image. 'But not only that, they were masked caged dancers so you never saw their faces but I loved watching them, the dancing was wonderful and they would often portray sex positions from the karma sutra which would get projected onto a huge screen. I guess to give people ideas. It was so well done, not really seedy at all, more artistic as they were still dancing, sort of yoga positions which makes sense now. Anyways, it was very impressive to watch.'

'Okay…' I say, not too sure where this is going.

'Well, it was *him*. The Shmoo!' Her eyes widen as she takes a sip of her drink again. 'I mean, Greg was the masked dancer. The Shmoo *is* the masked dancer.' She flings her hands up into the air by way of explanation. 'He recognised me when he moved in above Aloe Lovely and he said he near enough died on the spot that I'd seen him like that. He recognised me you see, and was too shy to come in in case we laughed at him. That's why he's been avoiding me all this time, he thought I recognised him and we were staring at him because of that.'

'Well, you were, weren't you?'

'I was staring at him because he was hot. I didn't put two and two together. I never realised he was the masked sex club cage dancer.'

'Oh lord. So why has he decided to tell you all of this now?'

'I guess we just clicked what with me knowing sign language and everything. I said I recognised him and he said he better come clean and tell me because it may all come back to me when he takes me to the yoga studio and he didn't want me to freak out.'

'Oh wow.'

'Yes, wow indeed. He's so lovely Lottie and he isn't even into that scene, thank God. He was just doing the dancing for the extra money.'

'Well, I guess it led him to the venue for his yoga studio which is cool.'

'Exactly, everything happens at the right time.' Willow nods as her eyes twinkle at her own new found, comforting mantra.

'Maybe. Hey just think, you didn't need to try and entice him in with fancy scarves, gloves and wallets, you could have just popped a cage in the front of your window with a funky mask.'

'Or put a peep hole in the front door,' she jokes. 'No. That would have scared him off even further, I'm sure. He's a sensitive soul, connected to the earth and other living things. I can tell, that's why that plant Lawrence got him flourished so well in his care,' she continues.

I chew on my lip as I asses my friend's new perspective on things. The old Willow, as zen as she was, wouldn't have been so open minded or open to trying new business ventures but perhaps the death of her mum has changed her. Made her more accepting.

Chapter 25

Coolsbay village centre has never looked so pretty.

Pastel bunting lines the high street as balloon arches, that have been placed outside every shop to match its colour scheme, bob about in the light breeze. All the shades of green and cream for Aloe Lovely, yellow, blue and grey for Emmanuel's clothes shop and pink and navy for the bakery. The smell of freshly cooked hotdogs and delicious sweet treats carry across the air and in through the open shop door and my stomach grumbles in anticipation and hunger.

A gurgling sound emits from my gut, sounding very much like water going down an old plug hole. Willow makes a sympathetic face and points to the fridge. I raise my eyebrows and shake my head. I'm waiting for the hotdog so I can slide a cheeky gherkin inside. She nods knowingly, the only person who knows and understands my one addiction. I've been addicted to worse things; alcohol and tarot readings to name a few so pickled gherkins isn't so bad as long as I have some chewing gum nearby.

♣ ♣ ♣

Today is the 1st of March. If it rains, we commiserate and if it stays dry, we celebrate. Today is about laying it all out on the table, honesty and kindness. Today is about redemption, to say how you feel and banish any negativity. Last year it rained all day and the people of Coolsbay really felt it. A shit year followed for everyone, me included.

'Do you think it will stay like this?' I ask Willow, as she faffs about rearranging the window display for the fourth time.

She pauses for a second to assess the sky. She points ominously to a dark grey cloud which has been fast approaching all morning then begins to vigorously blow air out of her cheeks as if she's trying to blow the cloud away. I glance around the shop; it looks gorgeous and we've made a dozen videos showcasing its new, improved look. Aloe Lovely has had a mini facelift at just over one-year-old.

'Yes,' she says, with a huge breathy smile. 'It's going to be just fine; I can feel it in my roots.' Willow points to her feet and I smile back, feeling warm and fuzzy from her enthusiasm but I'm not too sure if I'm feeling quite as confident as Willow is. 'Either way, we'll get through it even if it does rain, we always do.'

I smile up at my boss and friend and blink back an unexpected tear. Today is my last day in the shop and then it's on to pastures new, well sort of pastures new. I'll still be working with Willow, just more virtually this time, in fact I'll be working with most of the local businesses on the high street in one way or another when it comes to their social media platforms, including Lawrence and Greg. I've even managed to bag a client in Cornwall, a handbag shop whose owner is a friend of Kathy's.

I'm finally self-employed and doing something I love. It's terrifying but I'm doing it. It's funny how what you're supposed to do can just fall into your lap, like it's just meant for you. Your life's purpose, and if you had a choice you wouldn't have even picked it but it found you and it's just right. If I'd been told a year ago that this time next year I'd be single and starting my own business, I'd have laughed and then cried myself out of the room then probably asked where I was living and cried a little bit more when I found out I'd been backwards and forwards between my brothers and my parents. Yes, that's right, it was too awkward with Liam coming in and out of the living room with the added anxiety of Missy Temple turning up so I had to get out of there. But really I'm happier and freer than I've been in a long time and I won't be living with the 'rents for long because the savings are slowly mounting up again. Mum and Dad have said they'll help towards a deposit for rent if I need them to, the old Lottie would snap up that offer of help but I want to do this by myself, they've done enough for me and now it's time to stand on my own two feet.

My phone buzzes in my pocket and I pull it out to see a flurry of excited *WhatsApp* messages from Lydia and Kate in the uni group to say that they're fifteen minutes away on the train. My stomach tumbles through nervous excitement, I have to be honest with them today and tell them the truth about the reunion. I can't lie to my oldest friends any longer. It was all a sham, a sham to make me look better but what did it actually achieve? An image of Brandon on his knees with his pretentious ring dug out of the valleys of Mount Doom sears into my mind's eye. What was I ever thinking when I considered getting back with him? I hear he's in Bristol now, working on a reality TV show to do with disgruntled exes. How ironic. There are also six messages on the old housemate group from Kathy asking if the rain cloud has cleared yet. We hardly used the housemate group except to tell each other to get milk, most of the time we just left each other sticky yellow notes and stuck them on the fridge. Liam would sometimes write on the old milk carton or on the last piece of toilet tissue, sometimes he'd make little art displays out of the recycling. Liam would sometimes make the best bacon sandwiches and morning coffees. Liam had the best cheerful morning smile that instantly put you in a good mood. Don't think about Liam. Don't think about Liam and his piercing blue eyes and smooth, firm, milky skin, don't think about him, that sexy Irish, kind, lovely, smiley man. Don't think about him, Lottie, you absolute fool.

'Lottie, you tool,' my little sister says, as she shakes my shoulders vigorously, her perfect hair bouncing all around her shoulders. 'We've been waving at you from outside the shop and you're just staring at us like a complete dumbo, can you not see out from inside the shop?' She puts her finger on the window and rubs it hard making it squeak loudly. Willow and I wince.

'Enough with the name calling you, I thought you two had become good sister friends,' Dad says, resting a hand each on Maggie's shoulder and mine. 'Remember what today is all about,' he continues, pulling us and Mum in for a group family hug.

'Yeah, yeah, we're all meant to be kind, make amends and be honest with our loved ones and if the universe thinks we're worthy, as if by magic it won't rain and we'll have a good harvest. It's all just woowoo nonsense though, I mean how can how we treat each other have an effect on the weather. Everyone knows it's absolute rubbish,' Maggie says, folding her arms and rolling her

206

eyes in that way only defiant teenagers can.

'Ooooh I don't know, the year your mother was finally honest with me and told me how she really felt was the year that we had the best harvest ever.' Dad looks at Mum who gives him a little wink and squeezes his hand.

'Yuck,' Maggie, my sister squawks.

'It is true,' a voice says and I have to rub my eyes to see if it's really him, Ravi. 'High level vibrations can carry through into the weather, rain is good as is the sun but of course we don't want rain today as it could be merely a symbol of unhappiness, an excuse for re-birth. So please hold off until tomorrow.' He looks up at the sky as if talking to someone and crosses his heart with his hand.

'Ravi! You're back!' I squeal, as I rush over to hug him. He never did reply to my email.

'I am, but only for today, special day, special offer,' he says with a little head wobble, as he takes my hand with both of his. I glance down at his nails and am surprised to see them painted. They're emerald green and he's wearing rings, lots of them. They look strangely familiar.

'It's so nice to see you! Where have you been? And I still owe you money from helping that non-homeless man.' I cringe slightly but then remember that he may not have been homeless but he was definitely in need of a hot drink. He certainly appreciated the act of kindness even though I took back the samosas and called him a greedy git for feigning homelessness, the thought was there at least.

'My gift,' Ravi says. 'I do not need it, so you keep it and pass it on when the time is right.'

'Thank you. So what have you been up to?' I ask, as Ravi's dark eyes squint with a hint of mischief. Mum,

Dad, my sister and Willow begin to chat shop as my eyes fall to Ravi's perfectly manicured hands again and then back to his dark, glossy, tied up hair. He grins widely, then ever so slightly shakes his head before closing his eyes for a brief moment and opening them again.

The penny drops.

Could he be?

No!

'What the?'

But the hands, the hands are the same. And the hair, although tied up, is the same glossy darkness as NextlevelNyssa, my secret internet life guru. Ravi's eyes widen as he turns his head to see who is listening. I gasp as a glimpse of the tattoo confirms it. The Hindi writing, the same one that NextlevelNyssa has tattooed on her neck.

'Nyssa?'

'Shhhh,' Ravi says, putting a finger to his lips to silence me before speaking in a low voice.

'It wouldn't be the same if everyone knew, Lottie. My followers are at two million now and I make a good living showing people how to live a happy and prosperous life and not get stuck in a miserable rut but I prefer them not to know it's *me*. Fame hungry I am not, just happiness hungry, and that is all that matters.'

'This is brilliant, I love it,' I whisper, but without being able to hide the excited squeal in my voice.

'Thank you. I go back to Goa in a week so I'm just here tying up some lose ends. I wouldn't miss the Coolsbay festival for anything, plus I'm tempted to get my palm read by the woman who took my shop space. Is she any good?' Ravi looks at me expectantly. Surely he doesn't need his palm reading?

'Hmm, well my reading wasn't true but perhaps she

was having an off day. I know others who have been gob smacked by her accuracy.' I recall the customers chatting in the shop about how good their readings were. But if that's the case then how could she get mine so wrong? Maybe I'm destined and doomed to be single forever and the cards weren't working or she just didn't have the heart to tell me. I did get the death card. Either way, it isn't so bad being on your own, much better than being with a bully like Brandon.

'Hey!' Lydia and Kate come running into the shop and fling their arms around me. My old mates are here!

'It's so nice to see you both, I'm ecstatic you came,' I say, as I hug them both. 'Good journey?'

'A long one but we're here now,' Lydia says wearily.

'It's been a while but I just love this place, it's so quaint and cute,' Kate says, as Lydia's head bobs along in agreement.

A loud horn sounds making Lydia jump and everyone stops what they're doing.

'What's that?' she asks.

'It means that the party has started,' Ravi pipes up, as he takes a glass of champagne from Willow's tray that she's offering round to everyone in the shop, he nods his head several times then winces at the sharpness of it.

The atmosphere in the shop and on the street begins to hype up as the sound of the marching band can be heard as it makes its way down the road. Shopworkers and customers stand at their doors and watch the crowds follow the band down the high street. Once the marching band has passed, a parade of women dressed as mermaids dance upon a huge white float as *Sam Smith and Kim Petras, Unholy* blasts out of the speakers. The float has been decorated to look like a whale and the mermaids dance around a merman/sailor who is trapped inside a cage, looking like he's trying to escape. I look over at Willow to see if she's clocked it and her face says it all. It's The Shmoo back in his cage, where it all began for them. He wriggles his hips or rather his huge fin and their eyes lock as he passes us by, tipping his sailors hat towards her as he does so.

'Well, that was a sight for sore eyes,' I say to Willow, as I try to hide a smirk behind my glass of fizzy water.

'It certainly was and he can fill me up with his seaman any day,' she mumbles more to herself than to me.

Lydia's eyes widen and Kate almost spits out her champagne.

'Willow!' I say, before bursting into a cackle that Willow and the girls join in on. I check to see if Mum and Dad heard but they're deep in conversation with Ravi whilst my sister Maggie looks out pouting onto the high street. She'll be off to uni in September to study criminology, she's such a smarty pants. She'll be going off without her boyfriend, which is why she's feeling a little down in the dumps at the moment, coupled with uncertainty and nervousness of what's to come. Her eyes move towards me and I poke my tongue out before mouthing *proud of you* at her. She laughs and mouths *proud of you too* before her eyes begin to well up and she looks away. You'll be okay sis, I think as my eyes begin to well up too. You go girl.

'What?' Willow says. 'The tension has been building for far too long! All I do is think about him day and night, Lottie, it's completely exhausting. He's even more lovely now I've got to know him a bit better and normally that's not the case is it, normally they're a disappointment.'

'Normally,' I say, while secretly disagreeing with her because Liam was way lovelier once I got to know him but I guess I did think him a bit of an idiot beforehand so it's not really the same. 'You'll get your smooch with The Shmoo soon.' I pat her on the arm as my eyes swivel to the sky, the dark grey cloud hovers over the entirety of the high street and it's not looking good for a rain and pain free festival. Just as I think this the noise of someone shouting over a speaker about being proud to be a Coolsbayarian begins to take over the sound of the band playing. Another float comes into view closely followed by the booze party bike.

Oh. My. God.

The wacky Beau, Liam's friend, is standing up in the middle of the party bike on the boozy table whilst my old housemates, including Liam, pedal frantically around him. Laura, Beau's partner, steers. My heart skips a beat, it's been weeks since I've seen Liam and he looks better than ever, different but better. His hair looks longer and from what I can tell, he's pretty much clean shaven which shows off his strong jawline and beautiful neck. He doesn't look like one of those men that look odd when they've shaved off their face fur, almost like their mouths have disappeared, he looks annoyingly gorgeous and I've never wanted him more.

But I can't have him because his heart belongs to the witch bitch Missy Temple.

Chapter 26

'Oooh isn't that your delightful man?' Lydia says, as she points to Liam laughing with Harry on the booze party bike.

I feel a sudden irrational feeling of hurt, why didn't they invite me? But I guess I don't live there anymore. I'm out of the loop. Out of their lives but Harry would normally invite me, and Kathy and I have become quite good friends so it's weird of her not to say. Perhaps the situation between Liam and I is all too awkward for them and they feel they have to take it in turns to see each of us now.

'Yes,' I reply dreamily. 'I mean no,' I quickly correct myself. I must be honest now. The time has come.

'No?' Kate and Lydia say in unison, both with furrowed brows.

'Here,' I say, grabbing them another flute of champagne each. 'Let's go outside.'

'What happened?' Lydia says. 'You two seemed so into each other.'

'Yeah, I wish my husband looked at me the way *he* was looking at you,' Kate agrees.

'Well,' I begin, before taking a sip of my fizzy water. 'We never were.' I gulp and wait for their reaction.

'Never were what?'

'We were never together.' I close my eyes briefly, still embarrassed by my idiotic, ridiculous lie. Kate and Lydia gasp.

'But aren't you, I mean you're . . .' Lydia points to my glass and then my stomach. I look down.

'Oh god no! You think I'm pregnant?' I splutter, feeling my stomach with my free hand to check for myself. Nope not a baby in there, unless there is such a thing as an immaculate conception.

'Well, you weren't drinking at the reunion and we heard you ask for fizzy water earlier. . .' Kate trails off realising her mistake.

'I'm just not drinking girls that's all. Alcohol isn't my friend, we all know that. Drunk Lottie was a liability, horrible even and I've gotten used to having a clear head and I kind of like it.

'Fair enough,' Lydia says. 'So you were saying about Liam. . .'

'Yeah, go on…' Kate says gently as I let out a huge sigh.

'We were never together, it was all a façade,' I confess, before taking a big deep inhale of breath. 'I actually booked an escort to come with me but he ended up basically being Del Boy from *Only Fools and Horses* and there was no way I could bring him.' Kate and Lydia's hands fly up to their mouths but I continue anyway, needing to get it all out. 'He just wasn't the vibe, not suitable at all, so Liam, being my housemate at the time, kindly offered to come with me and pretend to be my other half. Mainly to make Brandon jealous and potentially win him back but in the end, I found wasn't what I wanted anyway. Really, I was just so embarrassed about my life, girls. I had nothing to show for the last ten years. No boyfriend, no kids, no career, no car, no home. I was desperate to prove I was worth something. And even if I didn't have any of those things, at least I could show that *somebody* loved me. Somebody who thought I was worth taking a chance on and then my uni friends wouldn't think I'd completely failed at life.' I squeeze my fingers tightly around my plastic glass, fighting back the tears.

'Oh Lottie, we're your friends, we don't care about all those things.' Kate flings an arm around my shoulder and pulls me in close. 'You're amazing without all that stuff. You're funny, kind and interesting, and don't let anyone else tell you differently.'

'Yeah, we didn't have any of that stuff at uni and we had the best time,' Lydia reminds me.

'Stuff is over rated anyway,' Kate pipes up. 'Especially kids,' she jokes.

'Yeah and husbands,' Lydia says, deadpan. She said the reunion gave her the guts to start taking care of herself and she couldn't look healthier and happier. Good for her. It's only a matter of time before the younger model that he traded her in for will be doing the same to him.

'Thanks girls, I wanted to make Brandon insanely jealous which sort of worked, but then it just made me feel horrible and I realised what a truly nasty person he is. He turfed me out so that he could go off travelling and get his end away with a girl in every continent and then expected me to just fall back into his arms when he got back. It was him who turfed me out, not his parents. He was such a shit.'

'I think he destroyed your confidence, Lottie,' Kate says gently, as she rubs my arm.

'I think he did,' I agree. 'But I'm okay now. I mean,

me and Liam aren't a thing, we were never really a thing but I'm happy, I really am. I feel free, and I've made something of myself. I've got a little business.' I smile through my tears, frantically trying to wipe them away with the sleeve of my top as the party bike edges closer to the shop.

'You've got your sparkle back,' Kate continues. 'I could see it at the reunion. It must have started to come back a little while after Brandon took off, it just took you longer to see it,' she says.

'Yes, your sparkle must have been reflecting off his Turkey teeth when you kicked the ring back in his face and chipped one of them,' Lydia quips.

Kate and I throw our heads back and laugh. She's right. Those teeth would probably glow in the dark. A frightening thought.

'And there's something else,' I confess quietly, turning away from the ever-nearing party bike. 'I do have feelings for Liam but it's all a mess and I can't really do anything about it anyway.'

'Well he's here now,' Lydia whispers. 'So you might want to get together a quick plan.' I gasp and stand frozen to the spot as I feel a hand tap me on the shoulder. Kate and Lydia smile at the person whose hand it belongs to and for a moment I want the ground to swallow me up.

Did he hear me?

'Hey,' Liam says, as I turn to face him, his lovely clean-shaven face taking me by surprise. 'We've got a puncture, well a couple actually, Beau ran over a load of sharp shells that must've fallen off the mermaid float, so we're not going anywhere for a while,' he says, as a man with a rainbow beard playing a flute skips down the road like it's the most normal thing in the world. 'We were going to pick you up as a surprise but the mermaids ruined the plan,' he continues, pressing his lips together. Kate and Lydia do a double take but my eyes stay on Liam, who I've noticed has a tiny scar along his jawline. So small that if he didn't have such clear skin and wasn't freshly shaven, and I wasn't so close, I may not have noticed it at all.

'Oh no, need any help?' I say, not sure what help I'd be, having never fixed a bicycle puncture in my life.

'No, it's fine, anyway I just thought I'd come and say hi anyway as it's been a while. Well, I best be off now, bye.' He offers a little wave and a smile before hesitating then walking off towards the party bike. Kathy and Harry stand chatting next to Beau who seems to be attempting to fix the tyres with some sort of kit. Kate and Lydia eyeball me before Kate mouths at me to, '*Just talk to him now.*'

'Umm Liam,' I say loudly, as Kate thrusts me forward like a little school girl. He turns back, offering another lovely smile. 'Fancy a walk down to the beach? Get you out of fixing the party bike?' I grin nervously as Beau shouts at and kicks a bike tyre in the background, calling it a fucking piece of useless shit at the top of his lungs while Harry, Laura and Kathy try to hide their amusement and offer help.

'Sure, that would be grand,' he says without hesitation.

Liam and I walk in silence down to the beach passing the long parade of floats and people. One of the floats which looks like it's been dressed up as Noah's Ark, toots its horn at us as we pass by so we both wave back at the people in a pair of elephant's costumes who are dancing next to a pair of tigers and wobbly looking giraffes wearing bowler hats. We pass the bakery and I clutch at my stomach as the smell of the food makes my mouth water. I haven't eaten anything all day apart from two pickled gherkins. Copious amounts of fizzy water, nerves and hunger combined has made me feel quite lightheaded. The noise of the music coming from the floats tingles loudly in our ears until it finally begins to peter off as we turn a corner down a side street, towards the beach. We continue to walk in a somewhat comfortable silence as I admire the well-manicured gardens of Coolsbay. Colourful tulips; snow drops and daffodils enthusiastically try to make an appearance in time for spring. They're so beautiful and so is he, I think slyly eyeing up his creamy coloured arm and toned bicep. I should say something now. I should say something. The silence is becoming quite deafening.

'So, what do you reckon? Will it rain today?' I ask, as I carry on watching my feet pad along the pavement, suddenly feeling too shy to look at him.

'Who knows,' he says, sounding a little distant. 'Anything is possible.' We get to the end of the street then pad down a narrow path edged with sand and grass. I stop to take my shoes off, desperate for some relief from these shoes and to feel the sand between my toes.

'If I'd have known we were going for a walk, I wouldn't have worn these ridiculous shoes,' I joke, as Liam lends me his arm to lean on as I take off my heels. Glancing up at him, my balance becomes unsteady as his face breaks out into the most beautiful of smiles. It's the kind of smile that says a thousand words. Has he forgiven me for whatever he thought I did? Can we be friends again? It would seem so. His smooth freshly shaved skin shows the hint of a dimple on his left cheek. My eyes drop to the little scar just above his jawline again. I catch my breath as the tarot card reader's words echo in my mind *'The reunion is coming and the escort will bear a scar on his jaw. Pay attention to the escort. The laughs will be plenty and new love is challenging but just around the corner for you.'*

I want to reach out and touch it, trace the length and roughness of it with my finger and ask him how it got there but instead I stay frozen to the spot like a rabbit caught in headlights.

It was him all along.

He was my escort.

'Are you alright?' he asks, tilting his head, his smile now fading, replaced with eyebrows knitted together.

'I um yes, yes I'm fine, just fine.'

'Come on, let's go down to the sea, it's fresh out there today,' he says, as I fight the urge to let my hand fall into his. I imagine my hand feeling small in comparison to his large slightly rough, manly hands as I knit both of mine together. We wander down to the sea, the wind blowing my hair wildly around my face like seaweed. Both of us watch the waves for a little while until Liam opens his mouth to speak.

'You look like a mermaid like that.' He moves my hair with his hands so that it's away from my face.

I smile, then remember myself. 'Liam, I think we have a few things to discuss.' I take a step back, psyching myself up to ask what the *craic* has been these last few weeks. His light blue eyes mimic the colour of the sea which is mirroring the now clear sky. Perhaps it won't rain after all.

'I know,' he says. 'And I should probably tell you that I'm leaving.'

'Leaving?'

'Yeah, so you can have your old room back, Harry said it would be fine,' he says, his voice sounding raspy.

'Great, well thanks. Going anywhere nice?' I sound

like a hairdresser asking where their client is going on holiday. I grin awkwardly at him. What the fucculent is going on?

'I'm travelling to Peru to help with disadvantaged children who get hardly any attention at home,' he says. 'It involves building and decorating the new youth centre whilst supervising the kids that choose to help out in the evening. The ones that have no place else to go.'

'Really? That's amazing! I'm so pleased for you, they're lucky to have you. When do you take off?'

'In two months.'

'Two months,' I echo.

'Yep.'

My eyes fall to study a small blister on my toe as Liam and I stand in an awkward silence for what seems like an eternity.

'Come with me?' Liam blurts out. 'They still have spaces, there's no fee as they're crying out for help.' His cheeks pinken. By the look on his face this invitation has come as a surprise to him too.

'What?'

'It's just a few hours away from Machu Picchu.' The git. He knows I want to visit there.

'Liam you… I… you haven't spoken to me for weeks and now you want me to come to Peru with you. What's going on? And what about Missy? Could she not make it so now you want to take me?' I scoff, sounding way more bitter than I intended to.

The cheek of him.

'Charlotte, Missy and I aren't together,' he says, searching my eyes. 'Just as much as you and Lawrence never were.' Damn you Harry and Kathy. 'Missy and I were doing business together, we had the occasional business meal but I've been told she told everyone else we were dating. It wasn't true. I was horrified when I found out what she was saying, embarrassed. She's quite awful, deluded even, but there wasn't much I could do, she was sort of my boss so I had to humour her a little, I needed the money to settle a few solicitors' bills. The house I had here was with my ex and we were selling it, long story but I'll tell you all about it if you want. That's why I came back,' Liam explains, not breaking eye contact the entire time. So that was the *and stuff* he came back to sort out. His ex. It all makes sense.

'I'm done with playing silly games, I've done all that shit and I'm not about to go through it all again,' I say, thinking of Brandon big dickhead energy and all the games he used to play with me. 'I'm done with all that. I don't need it,' I repeat.

'I know,' Liam says as he moves my seaweed dancing hair away from my eyes. 'It was a surreal moment for me, when you read the poem in the bath, it kinda dragged up loads of old feelings. I hadn't really spoken of my mother in such a long time but when we talked about her on the road trip, I thought it would be cool to read some of her poems but it just brought it all back and then I remembered what she said before she died...'

'And what was that?' I ask as I recall all the colour draining from his face after I dropped the book.

'She said that if I ever find a girl who I can truly be myself with, have real fun with, who laughs at my jokes but keep me on my toes by putting me in my place then I should never let her go. As a teenage boy I just shrugged it off but her words have haunted me every time I saw *you* since the road trip and probably a little before if I'm honest. It freaked me out. I didn't know how to act around you anymore. You're Pricey's annoying little sister, Grotty Lottie.' He nudges me with his shoulder.

'So you decided to ignore me instead?' I snap then fold my arms, avoiding all eye contact, feeling like a petulant child who's just been told she can't have any more sweets.

'I didn't *decide* as such,' he says, carefully. 'It just kind of felt awkward and you were guilty of ignoring me too,' he teases. 'I'm sorry.' He looks at me pointedly. 'So do you fancy an adventure? Another fun road trip?' He nudges me gently on the shoulder as he chews on his bottom lip. A road trip is definitely tempting but perhaps not with him.

'I've just got myself sorted with my career, most of my clients are here, it just wouldn't be feasible.' I shake my head before sneaking a glance at his expression. He looks broken.

I nudge him back with my shoulder and our hands clumsily touch, slowly intertwining. I study his bright blue eyes, vulnerable as my fingers moves to his face to trace the small scar along his jaw.

'How did this get here?' I ask.

'If I told you, I'd have to kiss you?' He brightens.

'How did it get there?' I giggle, as he suddenly pulls me closer to him, his lips now millimetres from mine.

'Oh, I fell off a chair, some feisty young girl pushed me when we were younger.'

'Oh really?' I say, as the image of him on our kitchen floor clutching at his face piques my memory. He was teasing me about something but Harry told Mum that it was him who punched Liam. Shit, it's all come back to me now, Harry covered for me because he had to go to hospital. I've scarred the bloody man for life!

'Really.' He nods.

'I'm so sorry.' I trace the scar again with my finger,

leaving my hand on his face. He shakes his head, laughing and I feel his hot breath on my palm. 'I probably deserved it to be fair and I've actually grown to quite like it.' He puts his hand on top of mine then kisses me quickly yet lightly on the lips. Tingles travel through my lips all the way down my spine and I resist the urge to throw myself at him as the hairs stand up on the back of my neck.

'Oh yeah?' I whisper.

'Yep, because now I will always have a little reminder of you, no matter how far apart we are,' Liam murmurs, as I close my eyes and allow myself to get lost in his passionate kiss. In a way I wish I could go with him but this time I have to focus on me. I've got to put me first.

Is this goodbye?

Or just goodbye for now?

I kiss him back and let myself get lost in the moment as the sun makes an appearance, warming up my face, increasing the feeling of euphoria even further. My body feels weightless and for a moment I forget all of my worries and concerns. I may not be going with him but in a strange way it gives me comfort to know that I'll always be a part of him and that makes me smile.

A lot.

Chapter 27

6 months later. . .

NextlevelNyssa
In order to level up you must let go of who you used to be and be prepared to go through a period of difficult transitions. Lean in to feeling uncomfortable, embrace it, after all growth only comes after pain. I want you to do something for me. Write down three things that you would like to manifest this year. Then write down why you don't deserve them. Trust the process. It won't be easy but it will be worthwhile, I promise.

1. *Own my own home – I really need my own space more than ever.* **On hold for the time being. Owning own space is overrated if you're happy in the company of the people that you share space with.**

2. *Find my purpose – or at least a full-time job that I like – I can't sponge off Willow forever. I'm not sure if she even needs a part-time shop assistant. I don't deserve this because I'm a flaky person who never finds joy in work.* **Exceeded and completed. Career accomplished. I am not a flaky person and I do enjoy my work, it just took me a bit of time to find the right work.**

3. *Get Brandon back – and make his parents see that I'm worthy of him. I am worthy of him.* **No. You are worthy of way more than him and his parents put together and anyway someone else proved you were worthy of all the love.**

I lean forward and put the pen down on the small table before taking the final sip of my mocktail. Slumping back down into the white and pink stripy hammock, I let my open journal rest upon my chest as the hammock sways buoyantly from the disturbance of my movement. My eyes close, allowing the hot sun to beat down on my face as I feel myself smile, enjoying this little piece of heaven.

When I initially wrote the list, I didn't put why I didn't deserve any of those things apart from the job, is that why that one wish worked? If that's the case then I'm glad I didn't acknowledge any limiting beliefs on the other two points or God knows where I'd be now, probably about to get my own set of turkey teeth with Brandon in preparation for our non-wedding? I shudder at the thought of the vile promise along with the vile ring he offered me before opening one eye and sneaking a look at gorgeous, beautiful Liam. He's gorgeous inside and out and he's now studying me from his blue and white stripy hammock. Coconut trees form a small amount of shade over his feet whilst the beautiful white sands and turquoise sea backdrop looks like we've just stepped into our very own painting of paradise. The strong afternoon sun beats down on Liam's pale skin and I chuck him the factor fifty to make a point. I'm looking after him, last time we were out in the sun like this he got so burnt it hurt to sit down afterwards. The backs of his legs were red raw. I told him he was so hot he was on fire and we had fun with the aloe vera gel later that night cooling down the backs of his legs and other places. A naughty but nice memory creeps into my mind and I bite my lip, feeling myself blush.

'What's the secret smile for?' he asks, leaning forward to grab his drink as the sun cream lands between his legs. We arrived in Goa a week ago after having completed our charity work in Mumbai. I didn't go with him to Peru but we enjoyed our two months together getting to know each other more and we kept in touch the whole time he was out there. He kept me updated with photos and messages and I longed to be with him but this time I had to put myself and my career first. That felt good, liberating, but it didn't mean I didn't miss him desperately so when he asked if I'd like to come to India of course, the answer was yes. It's been an eye opener to say the least but completely worth it and I wouldn't want to be anywhere else with anybody else. I feel we can achieve anything together. We're unstoppable and I can do most of my work from the comfort of my phone.

'Nothing,' I say, smiling back at him. 'Just doing a bit of self-reflection that's all.' I close my journal and make a mental note to make a new list later. Making planning another trip with Liam on the top of said list.

'Is that so, and what reflecting would that be?' It's been almost six months since Liam and I started speaking again at the Coolsbay festival. The rain held off on the first of March until the very next day which turned out to be a total wash out. Houses and shops were flooded and a fair bit of damage was done, Willow had to move most of her plants and stock up to Greg's apartment whilst her shop was sorted and by the sounds of it, the stock and plants have moved back down but *she* hasn't. She's finally got her Shmoo.

'Reflecting on my life and the stuff I thought I wanted

versus the stuff I've got so far.'

'Deep,' he says, taking off his sunglasses and turning his body towards me, the hammock swinging as he does so. 'And how does it fair so far, fine lady?'

'It's fairing pretty good,' I say, with a shrug and a smirk.

Liam grins and his blue eyes twinkle in the sun as he jumps out of his hammock and saunters over to mine. He slowly lowers himself down onto the edge of my hammock and we both laugh as it sways and bobs like a water bed.

'Oh yeah? Just good or better than good?' he says, before leaning forward and kissing me softly on the lips. Abroad Liam smells of cinnamon and coconuts and I can't get enough of him.

'Better, much better than good,' I murmur, before kissing him back. 'What was that?' I giggle as I feel a big splosh of water land on my forehead.

'I thought that was you drooling over me,' Liam jokes, as I lightly bat him away with my hand and sit up looking at the sky, holding my palms out to feel for any more splashes. Just moments ago, there wasn't a cloud in the sky and now there are several dark clouds hovering over us, which I guess isn't so different to life. You can be sailing along quite happily until something hits you and bang, life has changed forever. So you really should make the most of these times, savour every smell, feeling and taste, because you don't know when it could all change again.

'It is the monsoon, rainy season in Goa,' Ravi announces, as he appears with a tray of drinks. He carefully places them down on the small table between our hammocks then effortlessly glides off to get two umbrellas, placing each one over our hammocks to protect them from getting wet. We thank him as he studies the weather.

'This rain comes straight down.' He elegantly signals with his freshly manicured nails. Today they've been painted turquoise, with a sparkling diamante neatly placed in the middle of each fingernail. 'No wind. So you can stay here and watch it if you like. It's quite something. I feel as though it washes away all my worries, refreshing, invigorating. Gives my brain a good cleanse. In fact, I'm off to meditate in this, there's truly nothing better.'

Liam and I say our goodbyes to Ravi as we watch him climb the steps to his house, he drags out his little rainbow mat and places it on the veranda before sitting cross legged facing the weather.

'Penny for them?' Liam asks, as he scoops up a stray curl and places it behind my ear. I watch the big raindrops colour the decking, still not quite believing I'm here.

'It's just wild how my favourite corner shop owner became my favourite corner of the internet and now I'm here, in my new favourite corner of the world. I used to read Ravi/Nyssa's posts and long for his next piece of life advice and now I'm visiting him at his home in Goa watching him meditate on the mat I've seen in many an *Instagram* post.' I laugh and Liam treats me to a huge grin as his hand snakes around my waist and we both fall back into the hammock lying side by side. We giggle as the hammock sways and the rain ricochets off the umbrellas.

'It's wild definitely,' Liam considers. 'But also wonderful, because if it wasn't for him leaving the corner shop, I wouldn't have got to go with you to your uni reunion and have you fall madly and deeply in love with me.' He winks before treating me to another dreamy grin.

'Okay, but let's not forget that it was you who was

always waiting in the wings,' I tease back, as the memory of an uptight me eager to impress her peers passes through my mind.

'The backstory you came up with wasn't far wrong though,' he says, as I remember his protests to it being too gooey.

'No?

'No, it's true. I was always waiting in the wings.' Liam bites his lip and looks out at the rain. 'All those things I said at the bar about you when Lydia was upset about her husband were true. I didn't have to act any of that stuff which is probably why it was so convincing. It wasn't that fake after all.'

'That's so sweet,' I squeak, blinking back the beginnings of an ugly cry. I'll blame it on the Monsoon if he notices. It's just rain splashed on my face.

'I know,' he says, as he turns to face me and tenderly wipes away a rogue tear/raindrop. 'I think I've always loved you,' he says, as I make a face.

'You were awful to me as a kid and I broke your face.'

'You didn't break my face at all, and there's a fine line between love and hate. That's what I told those girls on our road trip.'

'The girls at the service station?' I ask, sitting up a little straighter.

'Yeah, they weren't going to give me their numbers otherwise so I told them not to worry and that I was in love with you and it was all part of the big plan to make you fall for me. I had big plans for the slave competition until my emotions got the better of me. One of the girls thought it was out of order to lie to you, but I assured them that when the time was right, I'd tell you how I really felt.'

'You sly fucculent,' I gasp before we both giggle at the

Willowism that's become a regular word in my vocabulary, a little piece of Aloe Lovely that'll stay with me forever.

'Yes but a sly love sick fucculent, I love you, Charlotte.'

'I love you too, Liam.'

THE END

From the author

Thank you so much for reading my book I really do appreciate it. I'm an Indie Author, part of a small family run imprint (Tamarillas Press) and not backed by a big publishing company. Every time a reader downloads one of my books I am genuinely thrilled.

If you enjoyed my book then please feel free to post your review on goodreads, Amazon or both. I cherish every rating and review, they really do make my day.

We've worked hard to eliminate typos and errors but if you spot any please let us know.
TamarillasPress@outlook.com
Belle Henderson

Belle Henderson

Belle Henderson loves to read and write. She lives with her family and her rambunctious beagle in Wiltshire. She absolutely loves hearing from readers so please feel free to connect with her via email or on social media.

Email: bellehendersonauthor@gmail.com
Instagram: Instagram.com/bellehendersonauthor/
Facebook: facebook.com/bellehendersonauthor/
Goodreads:
https://www.goodreads.com/author/show/18999602.Belle_Hend erson
Tiktok: https://vm.tiktok/ZMesW9RQA

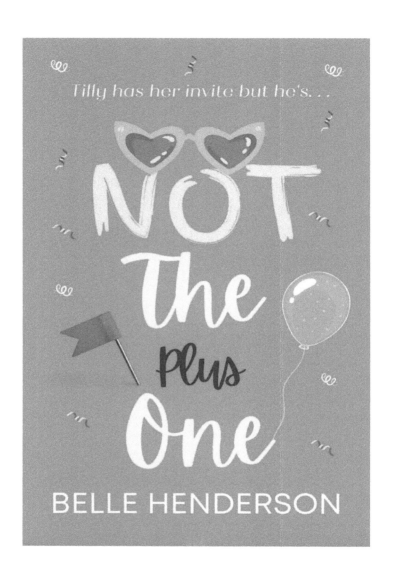

Tilly has her invite but he's...

NOT The plus One

BELLE HENDERSON

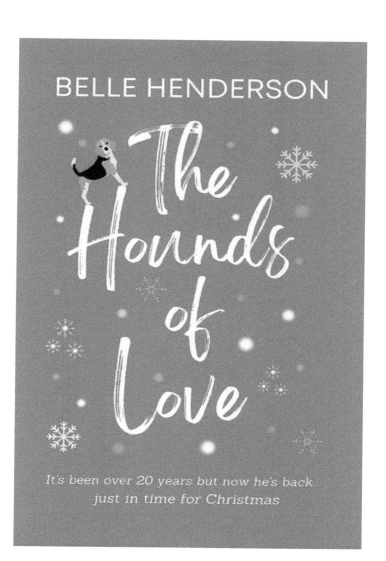

BELLE HENDERSON

The Hounds of Love

It's been over 20 years but now he's back...
just in time for Christmas

BELLE HENDERSON

What's eating FELICITY FROST?

A quirky tale of love, forgiveness and finding your people

BELLE HENDERSON

Livin'
La Vida
Lockdown

Life got hard but
then love got interesting

BELLE HENDERSON
& CJ MORROW

We
can
Work
it out

Two people,
one
opportunity

Ingram Content Group UK Ltd.
Milton Keynes UK
UKHW011822250423
420770UK00002B/129

9 781913 807337